For Arabella

THE
BLUE-EYED
ABORIGINE

ROSEMARY HAYES

F

FRANCES LINCOLN
CHILDREN'S BOOKS

'If we know how and where to listen, their ghosts may be heard as loudly and as clearly as the many other spectres that haunt Australia's history.'

And their Ghosts may be Heard,
Rupert Gerritsen

PART ONE

SHIPWRECKED

In Australia, the term 'an Aboriginal' is currently used to refer to an indigenous inhabitant, but in this book the 17th-century form 'Aborigine' has been used.

Chapter One

June 1629

Jan Pelgrom was miserable. He'd been a cabin boy for more than five years.

He spat on the deck. Nearly eighteen – and still a nobody. A puny, spotty, ugly youth with no chance of promotion.

His fair hair was the colour of mouldy hay, filthy and full of lice. He scratched his head, but it didn't stop the itching. His bare feet were black and calloused, his jerkin was stained and stinking, and his loose shirt and trousers were worn out and stiff with salt. On board, there was no way to wash your body in fresh water, let alone your clothes. Some of the sailors washed their linen in their own piss, but Jan didn't bother.

As for the drinking water – it was stale and full of tiny, wriggling worms. And it stank! You had to hold your nose before drinking it.

Jan couldn't wait for the voyage to end. He'd never thought he would miss his life in Holland and the crowded shack in Bemmel he'd shared with his large family. Bemmel was a long way inland, but he had always wanted to go to sea and he'd dreamed of serving on one of the great ships that sailed to foreign lands. He'd fulfilled his dream but it wasn't the romantic life he'd imagined. There was only the monotonous reality of life on board and he often found himself yearning for the windmills and dykes and big wide skies of home.

This voyage had already lasted for nearly eight months. They were sailing on the new ship, *Batavia*, from Texel in Holland to Java in the Indies, and everyone was bad-tempered. They'd been frozen with cold in the stormy northern seas, fried by the sun along the coast of Africa and buffeted by gales in the Southern Ocean.

Now, at last, they were in calmer, warm waters heading north again. Only a few more weeks to go, God willing!

'Cabin boy!'

Jan dodged away, as an older sailor cuffed him.

'Go and turn the sandglass,' he said.

Jan shook his head and muttered, 'I'm not on till first watch.'

The sailor grunted, and Jan moved swiftly away in case he was given an extra job.

Cabin boy! He smarted, and kicked out at the ship's cat as it slunk past him.

Jan made his way to the upper deck where the Commander, the Captain, the officers and the rich passengers lived. His next job was to empty the chamber-pots. He sighed. Unlike the crew and the soldiers and the poorer passengers, the people on the upper deck could use the two lavatories with wooden seats that jutted out from the stern. Jan couldn't understand why they needed pots in their cabins as well.

Emptying the pots was a foul job, and he often slopped them on his way to toss the contents overboard. He scowled as he passed two wealthy passengers, who turned away from him and shuddered.

'Stinking boy for a stinking job,' whispered one, just loud enough for Jan to hear. Jan lowered his eyes and said nothing.

Backwards and forwards he went with his pots of piss. He preferred being in charge of the sandglass – or even waiting at the Commander's table. That at least was clean work. But he wasn't often asked to serve at table these days. The Commander and the officers liked to see the younger, prettier boys, not a pug-faced, spotty youth like him.

But at least he didn't have to muck out the pigs and chickens any more. By now, all the animals had been eaten – or had died.

Jan took a moment to stand on deck and breathe in some fresh air. He knew the lines of *Batavia* intimately. She was squat and square-sailed with a prow hanging close to the water while her decks curved sharply upwards. She'd been new when she left Texel, but now the pale green paint and red-and-gold decorations looked chipped and weatherbeaten.

Jan yawned, and headed for his quarters on the gun deck. There was nowhere else to go between watches. He and the rest of the sailors lived there, spreading out their palliasses and sea chests between the huge cannons. As Jan climbed down the ladder, the smell that greeted him was overpowering – a stink of unwashed men, vomit and sweaty, filthy bedding.

As Jan made his way over to his palliasse, he passed a group of sailors huddled together in a dark corner. They stopped talking as he approached and waited for him to move away. It wasn't a happy ship, *Batavia*. People were always whispering in corners. The discontent seeped down from the top – from the uneasy relationship between the Commander and the Captain. Commander Pelsaert was no seaman. He was always unwell; and the Captain hated him.

But then, Captain Jacobsz hated a lot of people; it was best to keep well out of his way. He was an experienced sea captain but he had a vile temper, especially when he was drunk, and Jan was scared of him. Whenever their paths crossed, Jacobsz always scowled at Jan and, if he did speak to him, it was only to find fault. Luckily, Jacobsz only saw him when he had to serve at table or, occasionally, when he was turning the sandglass.

And Jan was becoming even more scared of the Captain – since an event a few weeks earlier.

Jan had been coming off watch after turning the sandglass. The moon was shining but its light was pale and at first he hadn't realised what the shape was, close to the ship's rail. But he recognised the smell, the unmistakable stink of human shit.

Then he had heard moans, and he'd stopped in his tracks and turned towards the sound. Someone was there, lashed to the ship's rail. He went closer – and then staggered back in horror. The stinking, huddled mass was Lucretia van der Meylen, a beautiful, well-born young woman. She was writhing and moaning, trying to free herself. What had happened? He'd edged forward again, and by the soft light of the moon he had seen that she was half-naked and that her private parts were covered with shit and tar.

Jan had only hesitated for a moment. He knew that Captain Jacobsz was behind this. He wouldn't have done it himself – he was too clever for that – but he would have ordered it – ordered it as an act of revenge. Jan had seen him making advances to Lucretia and he'd seen her rebuking him sharply when he touched her glossy hair and suggested who knows what.

Then, 'I'll get help,' Jan had muttered, and he had run to the Commander's quarters and pounded on the cabin door.

'The Lady, sir,' he'd shouted. 'The Lady Lucretia

has been hurt!'

Although the Commander was ill, he had come quickly, and by now some of the other passengers had heard Jan shouting and were gathered on the deck staring at Lucretia.

One of the sailors had untied her, and a woman had come forward with water and a blanket and had coaxed Lucretia to stand up. Then the woman had taken her below, half-carrying her through the silent crowd that had parted to let her pass. Jan noticed that Lucretia's long brown hair had been chopped short.

Just then, someone had held up a lantern and Jan had seen a smirk cross the Captain's face.

Captain Jacobsz was not a man to be crossed.

Jan sighed, and settled down on his filthy mat. For a while he thought about the brewing discontent on board and prayed that they'd reach Java before anything bad happened. Everyone knew that Jacobsz despised Commander Pelsaert, but he was friendly with one of the other Company employees – the Under Merchant, Jeronimus Corneliez.

Corneliez wasn't an easy man to size up; he was quieter than the blustery, ill-tempered Captain, but he had charm and authority. Now he *was* a leader, and together, these two men made a powerful force – Jacobsz the expert seaman and Corneliez the leader. But there was something else about Corneliez – something steely and cold, something about his eyes that seemed to look straight through into your soul.

At last, despite the noise and stench surrounding him, Jan fell into an exhausted sleep.

It seemed no time before someone roused him with a well-aimed kick. It was time to eat.

They ate from a bowl of rations issued by the cooks, each containing enough for six sailors. Jan took his place next to the carpenter, Tweis.

No one talked much. Everyone knew what they would be eating. The fresh food they'd taken on in Africa was long gone. All that was left now was pickled or dried: dried peas, pickled fish, pickled vegetables. And ship's biscuit, full of weevils.

Jan ate his food hungrily and winced, as he worried at a rotting tooth. He'd tried to pull it out but it wouldn't come.

'Your breath stinks,' said Tweis.

Jan grunted. 'No more than yours.'

Tweis turned to the man on his other side, one of the locksmiths, and whispered something, giggling. But the locksmith scowled and said nothing in reply. Jan looked up and caught his eye, but the man looked away. Jan shrugged. Best leave him alone. Everyone had their moods.

Their meal over, Jan and some of the other cabin boys were sent to the orlop deck where the soldiers were housed, and set to work cleaning their quarters with buckets of seawater and a mop. But nothing could shift the smell of unwashed bodies and stale urine.

Jan hated the orlop deck. The space between floor and ceiling was too low for a man to stand and the cramped conditions made the soldiers ill-tempered. Many were French mercenaries, going to protect the Company's fortress in Java. They were a tough lot and the tension that existed between them and the sailors had led to their being quartered in a different part of the ship.

At last Jan finished and went back to the gun deck to catch a few hours' sleep before his midnight watch.

One of the other boys would come and call him in time to take his post turning the sandglass and ringing the bell for the watch. The sandglass was the only way of telling the time on board and if a cabin boy failed in his duty, the consequences were dire. Jan had been a cabin boy for a long time and he'd been whipped often enough for his carelessness.

But this time he woke early. Something disturbed him. He lay dozing, enjoying the brief respite before work. And as he lay there, he heard whispering.

'What about the boy? Can he hear us?'

Jan tensed and lay completely still. He recognised that voice. What was *he* doing down here?

A short laugh. 'No. He won't stir till they come to wake him. Sleeps like a baby.'

Then some more whispers. Jan didn't catch exactly what was said, but he'd heard enough. Enough to know that, if he moved a single muscle or showed any sign of being awake, he'd be as good as dead. The voices grew louder again.

'There are plenty who'll be with us. We'll be a strong force.'

'What of Pelsaert? What shall we do with the Commander?'

Then that unmistakable voice again.

'Commander! Call him a Commander! He's useless! Can't make a decision. Sick as a dog most of the time... he's no leader! We'll drown the man.' There were murmurs of assent. And then the whispers died down and Jan couldn't make out what was being said.

At last, the meeting broke up but, as they were dispersing, there was that voice again, speaking very quietly.

'So, we're with the Under Merchant, then?'

'Aye. Aye, we're with Corneliez,' muttered the others. Then there was silence and Jan heard someone leave the group. The men whispered urgently among themselves – whispering that stopped when, moments later, one of the younger cabin boys came down to the gun deck. As usual, the older men cuffed the boy and made jokes at his expense.

Then the boy was at Jan's side.

'Your watch, Pelgrom.'

Jan didn't move. The boy poked him.

Jan groaned. 'Get off. I'm coming.'

He staggered to his feet and rubbed his eyes.

The locksmith looked up. 'You could sleep for the dead,' he said.

Jan nodded. He didn't dare look the locksmith in the eye, for his had been one of the whispering voices.

But the other, the harsh voice which had scared him. That had been the voice of the Captain, Captain Jacobsz. What was going on? The Captain *never* came down to the gun deck.

Jan looked round nervously. There was no sign of Jacobsz now.

Jan made his way thoughtfully along the passageway and up on deck. He was glad to get away – not just from the stink and the cramped conditions, but also from the edginess and suspicion that was brewing down there.

He walked across to the sandglasses which were mounted close to the ship's bell and not far from the whipstaff. Jan didn't mind turning the sandglasses. As long as you didn't forget to turn them the moment the sand had run out from top to bottom – that was the worst crime.

There were three sandglasses, one set to run out in one hour, one in half an hour, and a little half-minute glass. Jan's job was to turn the half-hour and the hour sandglasses. And every half hour, during his four-hour watch, he rang the ship's bell. Sailors were put on four-hour watches throughout the day and night, and the bell told the whole company where they were in the watch and when to change.

So it was one bell for the first half-hour of a watch, two bells for an hour, three bells for an hour-and-a-half and so on until, finally, eight bells for four hours.

And then Jan would go off duty and the whole thing would begin again. Another watch, another eight bells.

Jan enjoyed the first watch of the new day. It was a quiet time and he was only disturbed by a sailor coming in to use the half-minute glass and check the speed of the ship.

A gusty south-west wind filled the ship's sails and she sped forward. It was a clear, bright night and the moon revealed the shape of *Batavia* as she ploughed onwards to the north.

The hatches were battened down and the only light came from the moon and from the enormous lantern, five feet tall, which hung over the stern.

The first watch was the most difficult of the day. It was when men were at their least alert. This is why, Jan liked to think, he was often chosen for it. He was older than all the other cabin boys – more experienced. But it was also why the Captain often came up on this watch, to assure himself that all was well.

It was nearly 3 a.m., towards the end of the watch, when Jan heard the familiar sound of a small doorway opening. He tensed, his stomach knotting. Jacobsz!

But Jacobsz didn't bother with Jan. He went to talk to the steersman, before joining the sailor on lookout, and the two men watched together, their shapes picked out by the moonlight. Jan glanced up at them from time to time, wondering what thoughts were going through the head of the Captain. Why had he been down in the gun deck? Why had he been whispering with that group of sailors?

Jan started to feel drowsy, and he shook his head sharply. He glanced at the Captain, hoping those sharp eyes hadn't noticed his drooping head.

But the Captain was talking to the lookout. The other man was shouting and pointing, his voice urgent.

'There's white water ahead, sir!' he cried. 'Could be a reef!'

Then the voice of the Captain. 'Nonsense, man. It can't be. We're miles from land.' He laughed, and lightly punched the sailor. 'Why, it's just moonbeams on the waves, that's all.'

Then Captain Jacobsz left the lookout and went back to speak to the steersman.

'Hold your course,' he said firmly.

And so when *Batavia* struck the reef a few minutes later, she did so at full speed with all her sails set.

Chapter Two

There was a shuddering lurch as the great ship hit, followed by the sound of splintering timbers. The impact threw Jan away from the ship's bell and the sandglasses and on to the deck. His shoulder took the main force of the fall, and he gasped with pain and grabbed hold of the edge of a hatch to stop himself slithering towards the ship's rail.

For a few seconds all was still, with only the sound of the timbers groaning as the ship settled at a drunken angle and waves broke on the reef.

And then – panic. Shouts from below decks, footsteps running to see what had happened, sleepy passengers emerging from their cabins, bruised and confused.

Jan was throbbing all over. He looked up from where he was lying and saw the Captain towering over him.

'Stop cowering, you little runt,' he yelled, kicking Jan's side. 'Get up and see to the passengers.'

Jan didn't have to be told twice. He just wanted to get away from Jacobsz. And he had heard the Captain's command: *Hold your course.* He wished he had not.

He struggled to his feet, trying not to cry out in pain, and ran the length of the great ship to the cabins astern. All was chaos. Families were huddled together, sailors were running to and fro trying to help the injured, and everyone was shouting.

'What happened?'

'What have we hit?'

'Is the ship taking in water?'

'Dear God, we shall all die.'

In the gloom, Jan saw the young woman Lucretia standing motionless in a corner, flattened against the door of her cabin, her head bent. People shoved past her, pushing and jostling, but she stood, silent and unmoving. Even now, weeks after that shameful incident, the sailors avoided her, scared to be kind to her for fear of angering the Captain.

Jan gritted his teeth against the throbbing pain in his body. He felt sick and faint, but he also felt sorry for Lucretia. He knew what it was to be shunned.

He started towards her nervously, but just as he moved forward, a soldier came from out of the shadows and took Lucetia's arm. She looked up, and Jan saw her flinch at the soldier's touch.

'I won't harm you, lady,' said the soldier. 'You'll be safer in your cabin.'

Jan didn't know the soldier, but he was relieved that someone had gone to help the woman.

Lucretia looked at the soldier and smiled briefly.

There was so much confusion that Jan didn't know what to do. And then, over the screaming and shouting and swearing, he heard a strong, calm voice.

'There's no need to panic. The ship is holed, but the Captain tells me we are in shallow water. There is no immediate danger.'

It was the Under Merchant, Corneliez! He stood still, steady as a rock, his sharp profile clear in the moonlight as he calmly observed the chaos surrounding him.

Jan's shoulders relaxed. Thank God someone was taking charge!

And then Corneliez saw him. He looked him up and down briefly, then spoke.

'We need to check the cargo, boy. Go down to the hold and tell me what damage there is to the victuals and the valuables.'

Immediately, Jan's pain was forgotten and he darted away. When Corneliez gave you an order, you didn't question it.

But Corneliez called him back. 'Make a note of it, boy. Write it down.'

Jan stopped in his tracks and hung his head, afraid to meet the Under-Merchant's stare. 'I can't write sir,' he stammered.

'Oh, no matter,' said Corneliez impatiently. 'Use your eyes, and remember. Then come back and find me.'

As Jan turned to go he saw Corneliez's eyes following Lucretia's back as she went into her cabin and, even in the turmoil, Jan noticed the way he looked at her. It made him feel uncomfortable.

He hurried down to the hold. He'd never been there before. All the valuable cargo was there, together with the non-perishable food and the water. It was guarded night and day. But now, everyone had run off.

He found a candle and a tinderbox near the entrance. He lit the candle and crept around the vast area. As far as he could see, no water had come in, though some of the barrels and other containers had burst open with the force of the impact when the ship had hit the reef. But there was still food and water to be salvaged.

Jan went further into the hold to check the cargo. He had no knowledge of exactly what the ship was carrying, but he knew it was valuable and he'd heard rumours that it included gems, gold and silver, precious curios and fine cloth, among other things, to be traded for spices.

The first thing to catch his eye was the huge gateway which had been specially made to form a grand entrance to the Company's fortress in Java. It towered over everything, but it was securely lashed and hadn't shifted. Nervously, Jan crept among carefully-stacked chests, holding his candle. Here, too, the cargo had been thrown against the side of the ship with the impact and some of the chests had burst open. He saw a length of beautiful woven material which had been tipped from a chest and was spreading out over the floor. Gingerly he poked at it with his bare foot. Then he saw another chest whose metal clasps had flown open, and he lifted the lid and looked inside. Some rough cloth lay on top, but this had shifted, and Jan stared in awe at the gems underneath, their lustre brought to life by the candle. He put his hand in and brought out a few of the precious stones. God! What would these be worth? If he took just one or two, would anyone notice?

Then he dropped them back. These gems belonged to the Company. If he were found with them, he'd be shown no mercy. Thieving was severely punished.

Quickly he retraced his steps to the upper deck. As he emerged into the moonlight, he saw panicking passengers everywhere, shouting and screaming, with soldiers and sailors trying to calm them and make the stricken ship safe. The deck was full. There was no room to move and no one seemed to be in charge. The noise was deafening, drowning out even the noise of the surf as it pounded on the reef. Where was the Captain? Where was the Commander? And where, for that matter, was Corneliez, the Under Merchant?

Jan forced his way through the mass of people.

He must find Corneliez and tell him what was happening down below. He made his way to the Commander's cabin, thinking that they'd all be there – the Captain, the Commander and Corneliez – trying to decide what to do. But when he reached the cabin, his nerve deserted him. What if Corneliez were not inside?

As he hesitated outside the door, he heard raised voices inside. The Captain was there all right, and so was the Commander. The Captain was shouting but the Commander's replies were icily calm.

'This is your fault, Jacobsz,' said Commander Pelsaert. 'You cannot deny it.'

'The maps were wrong, man!' shouted the Captain.

'Nonetheless, you were in charge of the ship's navigation and I told you that in my opinion we were nearer the South Land than you thought. But you would not listen.'

There was silence then, and Jan imagined the two men staring at each other.

'Well,' said Pelsaert at last. 'What are we to do? What state is the ship in? Can she be repaired?'

'I have no idea.'

Pelsaert continued: 'Well you had better find

out, man. And if the ship cannot be repaired here, then we shall have to take the longboat and make for Java.'

Suddenly Jan felt a heavy hand on his shoulder. He jumped with fright, and spun round to find himself looking into the cold eyes of Corneliez.

'Eavesdropping, boy?'

Jan flushed. 'No, sir. I thought you were in the cabin. I came to tell you what's happening below.'

But Corneliez wasn't listening. He, too, had heard the angry voices coming from the cabin.

'The victuals, sir. And the cargo,' continued Jan anxiously. 'I went to check on them as you asked.'

Corneliez tightened his grip on Jan's shoulder and led him away from the cabin door. Then he gave him his full attention.

'Good. Now, tell me what you saw.'

Stuttering, Jan repeated exactly what he had seen.

When he had finished, Corneliez nodded. 'And you are certain there is no water taken on?'

'It seemed dry, sir.'

Corneliez frowned. 'What damage there is will be to her bow where she hit the reef, but when the tide changes, the water will rise. We must salvage what we can, but we must also lighten the load,' he muttered.

'Will you send men down there now?' Jan asked.

Corneliez glanced towards the cabin door. 'No boy, that is the Captain's job,' he replied sharply. Then he squared his shoulders, walked back to the cabin door and knocked.

Jan stood irresolute. Corneliez looked over his shoulder. 'Go and make yourself useful,' he said, then went into the cabin.

On deck, someone must have given orders, for ship's biscuits and brandy were being distributed to the passengers and things were a little calmer. A few minutes later the crowd parted to let the Commander through. Jan noticed the tremor in his hand and his pale skin. He had been unwell for most of the voyage and now he climbed unsteadily on to a coil of rope and began to speak. The crowd fell silent.

'There is no need to be afraid,' he said in a thin voice. 'We have hit a reef. The Captain will inspect the damage and see whether it can be repaired. Until then, we shall stay on board. Please allow room for the Captain and the crew to get on with their work.'

He coughed, even this short speech exhausting him.

'And what if it cannot be repaired?' This remark came from one of the passengers – the preacher, a nervous man dressed in black and surrounded by his wife and family.

Pelsaert took a deep breath, then pointed beyond the ship to where the pale light of the moon glinted on the sharp coral. 'As I said, we have hit a reef. But we think that the reef surrounds a group of islands to our east, so, if needs be, we shall make camp there.'

Now the Captain appeared red-faced and sweating, and started giving orders to the sailors and soldiers.

'Shift the heavy cargo and put it over the side. Come on, look sharp.'

'But surely the valuables will be lost!' shouted one of the passengers.

Jacobsz looked angrily at the speaker.

'We must lighten the vessel,' he said curtly. 'We shall have to see the damage, if we are to repair it.'

But the passenger wouldn't be silenced. 'And the Company's valuables?'

'We shall save all we can,' said Jacobsz. Then he squinted up at the huge mast which towered above them. He turned to a group of sailors.

'The weight of the mast will lock the ship more firmly to the reef,' he said quietly. 'We may have to cut it down.'

Many of those huddled on deck heard his words, and there were gasps and mutterings.

'We shall inspect the damage from the outside,' he said, louder this time. 'Then we shall know more.'

Jan saw a sailor with a rope round his waist climbing over the gunwale and being lowered down while other sailors paid out the rope. When the sailor was hauled up again, there was much gesticulating and shortly afterwards, one of the ship's boats was lowered over the side with an officer, the Captain and two more men in it.

The minutes passed, and dawn light began to creep over the scene. The crowd waited anxiously.

At last there was a commotion near the bow and Commander Pelsaert went over to talk to the men who had been brought back up on deck. There was a low murmuring, then Pelseart took up his position again on top of the coil of rope.

'It seems that there is a large hole in *Batavia's* bow,' he said.

Everyone started talking at once. Pelsaert held up his hand for silence.

'The Captain tells me that, for the moment, we are not taking on water, but when the tide changes, water will come in.'

More muttering.

Pelsaert raised his voice. 'Meanwhile,' he said, 'the Captain and some steersmen will take the yawl over to the islands to see whether we can make camp there.'

Everyone watched as the yawl was made ready and lowered into the water.

'Take care!' shouted the Captain, as the steersmen pulled away. 'There's only a narrow channel through the coral.'

Jan stared down at the reef. Jacobsz was right. The boat had to be lowered with precision or it would be holed by the sharp coral just beneath the surface.

Everyone on board watched as the boat made its cautious way towards the low, dark shapes which lay to the east.

Hours later, the yawl returned.

'Aye, there is land!' said one of the steersmen. 'Three small islands. They are all flat, and we could not tell whether they had water, but we can camp there until the ship is repaired.'

'Only three islands?' said Pelsaert,

'Only three nearby, but there seem to be others some way distant.'

Pelsaert nodded. 'Good. Then we shall make our home on the nearest large island for the time being.'

Jan watched the Commander. He was undoubtedly a sick man. He seemed to be forcing himself to stand upright and give commands. He pointed at a group of sailors.

'Tomorrow, at first light, you must transport people to the island. Women and children are to go first, with some men to protect them.'

It was an anxious night, and as the tide changed the ship began to take in water. As soon as dawn broke, everyone assembled on deck again. The preacher was standing close to Jan like some black crow. He was holding the hand of his youngest boy – a little toddler still unsteady on his legs – and the boy suddenly turned and smiled at Jan. Jan smiled back. He was unused to such friendliness.

Before long, the preacher's family were lowered into the first boat together with some soldiers. Barrels of water and biscuits and peas were loaded on with them.

Lucretia was waiting her turn to board. The soldier who had spoken kindly to her earlier stood beside her and helped her into the boat. Even though it was crowded, the other passengers moved away so as not to touch her.

Jan watched as the boat was lowered down jerkily to the water, and the sailors struggled to control it as they rowed through the channel in the reef. The heavily-laden boat lurched in the waves and the spray soaked everyone. Some of the women and children in the boat screamed with terror – but Lucretia remained silent.

All along *Batavia's* rail, people were watching and wondering. Among them was the Captain. Jan glanced at that harsh, knowing face and then quickly looked away. What was going on in his mind? The Captain knew this was his fault. Would he be able to repair the damage to the ship? Or did he have other plans?

Jan felt the Captain's gaze fall upon him and he

moved away, only to stumble into the solid figure of Corneliez, who seemed to have materialised out of nowhere.

'Careful, boy,' said Corneliez. His lips curled into a smile, but his eyes were dead.

'My pardon, sir,' muttered Jan, sliding out of his path.

'Boy!'

'Yes, sir?'

'You've done a good job these past few hours. Tell me your name'

'Jan, Jan Pelgrom, sir.'

'Jan, eh? Good, good.'

'Thank you, sir.'

Jan turned to go back to work. The Under Merchant had noticed him, had singled him out for special duties – had even praised him! He should have been flattered, but when he glanced back and saw Corneliez and Jacobsz whispering together, heads bent, he felt even more uneasy than before.

Chapter Three

All that day, supplies and people were taken from the ship to the nearby islands. Jan was still on board, but most of the women and children and many of the male passengers had gone, together with some sailors and soldiers.

The next morning, the sea was more turbulent and the spray came right up over the deck. Jan could feel the *Batavia* lurching under his feet and there was a ripping noise of timbers being torn from the hull. But he was too busy to be frightened, running here and there, doing odd jobs for the carpenters who were fighting a losing battle to repair the damage, as more and more water poured into the stricken vessel.

The Captain had ordered the main mast to be cut down, and he himself struck the first blow with an axe. Everyone left on board watched intently as each blow sent a shudder through the whole ship. Now the huge mast lay across the deck of the crippled ship.

For two days, people were shuttled past the first island to the larger one beyond, together with whatever casks of food and water could be salvaged. On and on it went, the longboat and the yawl ploughing back and forth until some two hundred souls were marooned on the largest of the nearby islands.

And then everything came to a standstill.

Jan had expected to be one of the last to be taken over, and together with some seventy soldiers and sailors he waited on board the creaking vessel for the longboat and yawl to return. But the hours went by and the boats didn't reappear.

As darkness fell, there were mutterings from those who were left.

'What's happened? Where are the boats?'

'Perhaps they are searching the coastline. Perhaps they are looking for a better place to make camp – some place with a good water supply.'

'Surely they won't leave us here?'

Not only had the boats gone, but the Commander's cabin was empty. He had disappeared, along with the Captain and several other officers and sailors.

Several days passed, and those on board stared out despairingly over the water, but there was no sign of the boats. Some still insisted that the Commander would never abandon them and that he must be searching for a water source, but others cried: 'He has deserted us. He has left us to our fate, God damn him.'

On board, the men were getting unruly. Jan, too, was desperate – desperate with thirst – and he was thinking of braving the chaos below decks to check the water barrels, when one of the friendlier soldiers walked by him – a man called Weibbe Hayes, who always acknowledged Jan when he was sent to clean the orlop deck.

Timidly, Jan asked if there were still barrels of water in the hold.

Weibbe blew his nose on his hand and wiped it on his trousers. 'Well, young Jan, you can go and take a look, if you dare, but those damned soldiers are running wild down below. I've tried to reason with them, but they're past caring. They've cracked open some of the wine barrels and they're all mad with drink. They've broken into the gun store and armed themselves, too.'

Then Weibbe took a leather water bottle from the wide belt which crossed over his shoulder. He held it out to Jan.

'Drink, lad. Not too much, mind. This may be the last I can get.'

Jan stammered his thanks, and gulped down a few mouthfuls of the stale water.

Weibbe took the bottle back and put a hand on Jan's shoulder, before moving off.

Jan watched him go. If even Weibbe couldn't control the soldiers, then he certainly wasn't going to venture below. In any case, he preferred to stay up on deck – even though up here it was a ghost ship, with all the sounds of daily life, the shouts of the sailors working the sails, the constant footsteps, the chatter of passengers, all nothing but an imagined echo coming through the sounds of the screaming gulls and the creaking of the ship's timbers.

As far as Jan knew, the Commander and the Captain were out there in the sea somewhere in the ship's boats. *Batavia* lay at a dangerous angle and Jan knew that they must abandon it soon.

Despite the best efforts of the carpenters, she was breaking up.

But how could they get away without boats?

Some of the sailors and soldiers had made rafts from the loose timbers and launched them into the sea. Some had clung to driftwood and floated away. And some had simply leapt into the water, intending to swim to the island. But the coral was sharp and could tear your skin to ribbons. And the islands were a long way off; only the strongest swimmers would survive. Jan had already seen several men drown. The waters here were full of swirling currents that could spin a man round and suck him under.

Jan was bruised, hungry and thirsty. He could hear the water slurping underneath him in the belly of the ship and most of the drunk soldiers had come up higher, lurching about on the deck, swearing and lashing out at anyone in their path.

As the sun sank that night, Jan propped himself up on the coil of rope which, only a few days ago, the Commander had used as a platform from which to address the crowd. He had no idea of the time. There were no watches to tell the sailors where they should be.

'Jan!'

His head jerked up, recognising in an instant the voice of Corneliez, and he started to struggle to his feet.

The Under Merchant approached him and Jan saw that he had one of the lengths of cloth from the hold flung over his shoulder.

'Not many of us left now, Jan,' said Corneliez, and when Jan didn't reply, he went on, 'There's no hope for the ship, you know.'

Jan looked up. 'What will happen to us, sir?'

Corneliez smiled, and Jan met his eyes briefly, but then he looked away. There was a glitter in them that alarmed Jan. Corneliez folded his arms and looked over Jan's head towards the islands.

'The Captain and the Commander will, no doubt, decide what will happen to us,' he said. 'I believe that they have made camp on one of the other islands with some of the soldiers and sailors.'

'On one of the other islands? Not where all the passengers are?'

'No.'

Jan frowned. 'Then who is in command where all the people are?'

'Who indeed?' said Corneliez grimly.

'Will you go there, sir?' asked Jan.

'Yes, Jan,' said Corneliez, shifting his weight and moving closer. 'I shall go there.'

'When the boats return?'

'Yes, when the boats return.'

Jan blushed. No one important had ever spoken to him like this before, as if he was worth something. Even at home in Holland, his mother had hardly bothered with him, and she had been delighted when he had found work as a cabin boy and she had one less mouth to feed.

Suddenly there was a shout from one of the sailors.

'The Commander!'

Everyone on the deck stopped what they were doing and stared. The ship's long boat and the yawl were heading past the reef.

'He'll be going to the island at last,' said someone. 'He'll be taking command.'

'Not before time,' muttered another.

Corneliez said nothing. He shaded his eyes and watched carefully.

But the boat did not head for the opening in the reef. It headed north.

Someone was waving from the boat and shouting.

'Pelsaert!' said Corneliez, his face expressionless.

'We can't hear what he's saying, sir,' said one of the sailors.

'No need for words,' said Corneliez. Then he added, 'The traitor.'

Only Jan, who was standing close beside him, heard those last two words.

Those left on deck continued to stare after the long boat.

'The sides have been built up,' said a sailor.

'Aye,' said Corneliez, 'You know what that means, don't you?'

The sailor nodded grimly. 'It means the boat is set for a long journey.'

Corneliez stood absolutely still. Then he laughed, making Jan look up.

'Well,' said Corneliez, 'He won't get far in that boat, built-up sides or not.'

Addressing no one in particular, he went on, 'He leaves us to our fate. So be it.' And he rubbed his hands together, the knuckles cracking. He seemed in high good humour.

'Carpenters!' he yelled. 'I need carpenters to make more rafts.'

For the next few days, there was banging and sawing and swearing as the carpenters tore out wooden planks from the ship and built rough rafts. They were racing against time. It would not be long before the sea claimed *Batavia*.

The next morning, one by one, the rafts were lowered down into the sea. Jan felt sick as he watched. The rafts bobbed about in the water, swept hither and thither like toys, sea spray soaking the sailors who clung on desperately to the sides.

At last it was his turn. He was pushed forward and told to lie flat on the raft as it was lowered.

But nothing could have prepared him for what was to follow. As the raft was let down, it bumped and scraped against the hull of the ship. The impact was so sudden that one of the sailors with Jan lost his grip and, after scrabbling wildly for moment, he fell off, screaming.

Jan didn't dare look down. He needed all his concentration just to hold on.

And then, at last, the raft hit the water with a great splash – but it was still attached to the ropes and crashed into the side of the ship again, swamped by a wave. Once, Jan was under water for so long that he thought his lungs would burst, but the raft surfaced just in time for him to take great gasping breaths before the next wave hit it.

One of the men on the raft with him was Tweis, the carpenter.

'Hold on for your lives!' he yelled.

Tweis. Even in his terror, Jan remembered that the carpenter was one of those who had sworn allegience to Corneliez.

Aye. We're with the Under Merchant. We're with Corneliez.

Above them, Corneliez loosed the ropes on deck, and immediately the raft plunged into the sea and was swept away.

The swell pulled the flimsy raft this way and that, tossing it about until Jan felt sure it would break up before they reached the island. Some of the sailors had lashed themselves to the raft with ropes so that they could paddle using the rough oars made by the carpenters. They tried to steer the craft towards the narrow channel through the reef, cursing and shouting when they weren't choking from the salt water they were swallowing.

On and on the journey continued, with the coral island still maddeningly distant. There were moments when the water was calm, when Jan raised his head to see what progress they had made, but then the swirling current would pick them up again and he had to lie flat, with closed eyes, and cling on until every limb screamed with pain and his hands lost any feeling.

All that day they drifted, tossed at the whim of the sea and wind. The man beside Jan moaned all the time and Jan became used to the monotonous sound, hour after hour. Then, as the sun was setting, the moaning stopped, and Jan risked a glance at his companion. The man's grip on the raft had loosened; he was too weak to cling on any more. Gradually, he slipped off the raft into the sea, and no one tried to save him.

By dawn the next day they were in sight of the larger island, but when they came closer the sea grew wilder and the sailors, weakened by hunger and lack of sleep, couldn't control the raft.

'We can't steer her!' shouted one, and with numb, fumbling fingers he began to undo the ropes that lashed him to the planks. The other sailors did the same.

'We're going to be thrown on to the coral!' they shouted. 'We'll have to swim for it.'

Swim? Jan couldn't swim.

Suddenly the raft hit something under the water. It flipped over, sending Jan and his fellow passengers flying into the sea. He felt the water close over his head and he tried to strike out with his arms – but they were too stiff.

Down he went. Down and down, spluttering, his lungs bursting.

I am going to die, he thought. *Drowned like a rat.*

He couldn't hold his breath a moment longer and he took a great gulp of sea water. His head felt light and everything slowed down...

All at once a sharp pain in his leg registered in his fuddled brain. He kicked out feebly and his foot struck something sharp and solid. He pushed on it, and gradually he started to float upwards again.

His head shot out of the water and he coughed up sea water. But, thank God, there was something underneath his feet now. He could stand up.

All round him he heard cries.

'Crawl over the coral!' shouted someone.

'Keep the raft. We'll need the wood.'

Jan couldn't tell whether the sailors with him were shouting, or whether the yells came from the island. He was so stiff and cramped that he could hardly move, his ears were full of water and his eyes were blinded by the salt. And he had gulped down quantities of salt water which he was vomiting back into the sea.

He staggered forward, tripping and righting himself as the coral cut his feet, until at last, bleeding and exhausted, he reached the shore and joined his companions.

The raft had broken up, but Tweis had dragged some of the timbers out of the sea and he stood beside Jan, breathing hard from the effort. No one spoke. They were breathless and battered.

Jan rubbed his sore eyes and tried to open them, but they stung so much that it was a while before he could focus on the scene before him.

They were standing on a small beach of ground coral. Jan blinked, and through blurred vision he saw that the island was a poor sort of place, flat and unwelcoming, with a few scrubby, windswept bushes dotted here and there.

Then he looked further and saw, huddled back from the shore, a silent mass of people. There must have been well over a hundred in the crowd but no one shouted out or welcomed them. They just stared.

The others from Jan's raft were staring, too.

Jan turned to Tweis. 'They're so quiet. Why are they not speaking?' His voice was hoarse.

Tweis shrugged, and they all staggered forward on to the beach. Jan's body was gripped by a spasm of shivering from shock and cold and he found it difficult to control his limbs.

Then he saw a figure break away from the crowd and come forward to greet them. Jan recognised the black clothes of the preacher.

One of the sailors spoke. 'We need water, sir. Where are the water barrels?'

But the preacher shook his head and when he answered, his voice was no more than a whisper.

'No water,' he croaked. 'We had but a few barrels and they are empty now. We are forced to drink our own urine. Pray God it rains soon, or we shall all die.'

Tweis had come up behind Jan. He stared at

the preacher in disbelief. 'No water?' he repeated.

Jan and Tweis looked round them. There was a menace about the silent island – a silence broken only by whimpers from the children huddled together in the crowd watching the new arrivals come ashore. Jan spotted the rest of the preacher's family and he was glad to see that the young boy – the toddler who had smiled at him – was still alive. Yet he looked listless; they all did.

Tweis questioned the preacher again. 'Is there no food, sir? What of the peas and biscuits?'

'We are trying to share those out,' croaked the preacher. 'And there are seals which the sailors and soldiers are killing for food, but we cannot survive without water.' He let out a sigh.

'Who is in charge, sir?'

The preacher made a sweep with his hand. 'We have a Council,' he whispered. 'Myself, the surgeon, some of the officers...' Then he stopped, the effort of speaking too much for him.

Jan looked back to the distant *Batavia*. The ship lay right over on the reef now, her severed mast pointing towards them accusingly.

Pray God that Corneliez will be saved, thought Jan. *Pray God that he will come. He will know what to do.*

He will take charge.

As Jan walked among the crowd, he met only fear from the passengers and hostility from some of the sailors and soldiers, who had been drinking from a wine barrel. He heard whispers from the passengers. 'Where's the Commander when we need him? Where's Pelsaert?' And another: 'And where's the Captain?'

Jan noticed that Lucretia was sitting quietly in the shadow of a rock and some of the children were by her side. Not far away was the soldier who had helped her on deck. Jan had found out his name. It was Wouter Looes. There was something about Wouter which was different from the other rough soldiers. Jan moved nearer to him.

'Any news of the Captain or the Commander?' asked Wouter.

Jan nodded. 'We saw them yesterday. They have taken the long boat and the yawl.'

Wouter looked up sharply. 'They have taken the ship's boats?'

Jan nodded. 'The Under Merchant thinks they have set off for Java to seek help.'

Wouter's eyes widened. 'For *Java*? In the long boat? They'll never make the journey in that.'

He hesitated, then went on. 'And the Under Merchant? What of him? What of Corneliez?'

'He stayed on board,' said Jan. But he promised he would come.'

Wouter looked across at Lucretia. 'If we don't get water, we shall all die,' he said. 'We need to salvage more water from the ship before it is too late but we have no boats, only some flimsy rafts.'

Jan glanced back towards the reef, and shuddered as he thought of how many had been drowned in that treacherous water. It would be a brave man who tried to make the journey back to *Batavia* on a raft.

Along the beach, Jan saw a group of soldiers and sailors. They had just slaughtered a seal and were hacking at the flesh and drinking the blood of the animal. But they were wild-eyed, and it was clear that they weren't going to share any of their kill.

Jan stood uncertainly at the edge of the crowd. All his life he'd been subject to discipline and now, suddenly, there was none. The Captain had gone, and the Commander, and many of the officers.

'Corneliez will come,' he said firmly to Wouter Looes.

But Corneliez did not come. For two more days Jan stared at the wreck of *Batavia*, hoping to see some sign of life, some movement, but the stricken ship kept its silence.

The next evening, it rained. Great torrents fell from the sky and suddenly the whole island was alive with every able-bodied person collecting rainwater in whatever vessel they could find.

The preacher walked among the crowd, his face upturned.

'Praise God, who has answered my prayers,' he said to anyone who would listen.

One of the sailors shoved him hard. 'Stop mumbling your prayers, preacher,' he said, 'and make yourself useful. Collect some water in that tall hat of yours.'

There were guffaws of laughter from his companions. Jan kept quiet. On board ship, the sailors would have been flogged for such impertinence.

That night, Jan slept on the damp sand surrounded by strangers. Families tried to keep together, mothers and fathers protecting their young like so many animals.

Some of the sailors and soldiers had found another barrel of wine which had floated ashore with countless pieces of driftwood and was – incredibly – undamaged. They had made quick work of emptying this down their throats and now were rampaging among the passengers, trying to force themselves on any woman who was unprotected. All night Wouter Looes stood sentinal near Lucretia.

Jan woke at first light, stiff with cold and still bruised and sore. The previous day, when the rain came, he and some others had found the bottom of a barrel and collected rainwater in it. A group of them were sleeping around it, guarding it jealously. As Jan crawled towards it, one of the others growled and pulled out a knife, but he relaxed when he saw Jan.

'Oh, it's you, cabin boy. Well, see that you only have a little. God knows when it will rain again.'

Despite the rain, water was still scarce and what food supplies were left were salted or dry, only serving to increase everyone's thirst.

Not knowing what else to do, Jan wandered away to look over the island. It was a low-lying, barren place with only a few scrubby plants growing in the sand and shale. Again his thoughts went back to his home land, the verdant green of the grass and trees, the fields, the windmills, the solid houses – and clean water everywhere.

As he came over to the other side of the island, he saw the familiar, dark-clad figure of the preacher, holding a book and intent on his prayers. Jan was about to turn away when the preacher saw him.

'No good looking for food or water over here, cabin boy,' said the preacher. 'We have already searched every nook and cranny of this island and there is naught to eat but seals and a few fish and birds. No fresh water anywhere.'

Jan trailed back down to the seashore and looked across again at the wreck. The sun was fully risen now and what was left of *Batavia* stood out starkly against the blue sky. The sea was calmer today and there was not a cloud to be seen – no hope of rain today.

Then he frowned and shaded his eyes with his hand. Was that someone moving on board? He stared so hard that his eyes ached, as he picked out a tiny figure and followed its progress as it clambered down over the gunwale, dangling on a rope.

Corneliez! It must be. He was the only man left on board.

Jan's spirits soared. He was coming, just as he had promised. But would he survive? Pray God he would not drown!

He ran back to tell the others what he'd seen, and all those who could move hurried to the shore. Some of the sailors and soldiers who had behaved so badly started muttering among themselves. Jan thought they'd be nervous of any authority, but they seemed pleased that Cornieliez was coming.

They all watched as the tiny distant figure hit the water and then was lost to sight.

He will have to be strong, thought Jan. *Only the strongest of men could battle with the treacherous rips in the water.*

Jan knew that Corneliez would be out of sight for hours – for days. Maybe for ever. He might never reach the island alive.

But even so, he continued throughout that day to stare towards *Batavia*, straining his eyes in the hope of catching sight of the Under Merchant in the water. He had never been one for prayers, but he found himself asking God to save the Under Merchant's life. Again and again, he muttered, 'Please God, save him. Let him live.'

The light faded and darkness fell, and at last Jan curled up on the sand. But he slept little that night and at first light he was down on the shore again, watching, waiting.

The sun had already climbed high in the sky when Jan spotted him. He was closer now, and Jan saw that he was sitting astride the bowsprit, using another piece of driftwood as a paddle. He was making progress, but it was very slow. Again Jan prayed that he would not drown, that he would have enough strength to cling on.

A few people gathered to watch with Jan and the news spread round the island. Soon there was a crowd on the shoreline, but Corneliez had disappeared. They waited silently and people began to disperse, thinking he had drowned. Then suddenly a sharp-eyed sailor called out, 'God be praised, he's alive!' And the crowd followed the direction of his pointing finger.

There were cries of encouragement from the onlookers.

'Keep going, man!'

'Have strength. You are nearly there.'

Then Corneliez lost his grip on the bowsprit and the crowd watched in horror as his body was pulled forward by the waves, tumbled and tossed and battered against the coral. But at last he lay spread-eagled, face down in the shallows. Several men rushed down to him and dragged him up on to the beach.

At first he lay as if dead and the crowd went silent. Then, slowly, he reached out a hand and a roar went up.

'God be praised, he is alive!'

'Give him water.'

Someone found a little water and took it to him.

Corneliez looked up at him. 'I need more than this, sailor,' he whispered. 'I've swallowed half the ocean. Where are the barrels?'

No one answered.

A sailor helped Corneliez to his feet but he swayed and his knees buckled under him. The crowd started to back away. Only the preacher came forward.

Jan watched the two men talking – the preacher gesticulating helplessly, Corneliez, kneeling on the ground, listening in stony silence.

'Help me to my feet,' said Corneliez at last, and the preacher hauled him upright.

'Listen to me, people,' said Corneliez, and, even though his voice was cracked, Jan's neck tingled at the authority in that voice. 'The Captain and the Commander have taken off in the long boat, so I am the senior representative of the Company. I am taking charge here.'

'We have already appointed a Council,' said the preacher quickly.

'A Council? Good. That is good. When I am recovered, we shall meet.'

There were mutterings of assent from the passengers.

Now that Corneliez had arrived, even the unruly soldiers and sailors were silent. Jan looked across at them. Had they all been part of the Captain's plot? Had they all said those words: *'Aye, we're with the Under Merchant'*?

Chapter Four

It was some time before Corneliez recovered his strength, even after receiving more than his fair share of the remaining victuals. Once revived, he set about organising the shipwrecked people and when he was not conferring with the Council, he walked about the island. Although he acknowledged the passengers, it was to the soldiers and sailors that he paid most attention. Jan watched as he spoke to some of them who, Jan knew, had pledged their allegience to him. What was he saying to them? Whatever it was, Jan could see that they were nodding in agreement. They were his men.

The next few days were a frenzy of activity. After all the rioting and drunkenness, there was at last some order. Every able-bodied crewman was ordered to drag driftwood from the sea as it came hurtling towards the shore. All sorts of strange objects floated in with the tide: more and more timbers as the ship continued to break up, as well as barrels, ship's furniture, chests, muskets and the personal possessions of both crew and passengers.

Corneliez ordered that everything except driftwood should be brought to him for inspection and that all the wood should be taken to the ship's carpenters to make larger vessels which could be rowed back to the ship to salvage supplies. He also ordered that what water they still had should be saved and used sparingly, though the carpenters were given double rations both of water and of seal's blood whenever a seal was captured. Tweis was kept busy from dawn to dusk. Supplies of nails and tools had been brought over earlier, before the Commander had left with the longboat and the yawl, so there was a constant noise of hammering and sawing and cursing as the carpenters put together a couple of makeshift boats.

As Jan was watching the carpenters at work, he noticed something metallic shining in the sand. It was the small bell used by the Commander to summon the cabin boys. Jan was surprised that it had not sunk. He picked it up, and saw that it was still attached by a chain to its wooden base.

He took it proudly to Corneliez.

'I found this on the beach, sir,' he said.

Corneliez turned from what he was doing and gave Jan his full attention. 'Ah, Jan,' he said, taking the bell from him and inspecting it carefully, 'Good. We can use this.' Then, as Jan turned to go, he continued, 'You shall ring that bell every time I have an announcement to make.'

Jan blushed with pleasure and his spirits lifted. Corneliez remembered his name!

At last the first of the new boats was ready. It was cobbled together from driftwood that had broken away from *Batavia* and been washed ashore – wood of all shapes and sizes. The carpenters had done their best, but there were no long, even timbers from which to make a smooth hull, and the craft looked very strange, with odd lengths of wood – some of different widths – patched together and overlapping one another. The rowing paddles, too, were roughly hewn from more solid pieces of wood, and splinters still hung from them.

The boat looked bulky and misshapen, but when the sailors tested it on the water it proved seaworthy.

And it was large – large enough to carry plenty of passengers and plenty of what could be salvaged from *Batavia*.

'Jan!' shouted Corneliez. Jan immediately scuttled to his side. 'Fetch that bell, Jan. I want to make an announcement.'

Jan came back with the bell and stood beside Corneliez, ringing the bell for all he was worth.

Everyone gathered round.

'We are to launch our new boat,' announced Corneliez, indicating the rough vessel that was bobbing about in the waves. 'But its first voyage will be to the two islands to the north.'

There was a muttering in the crowd. 'To the north?'

Corneliez went on. 'As you know, the Commander and the Captain, together with selected soldiers and sailors, took the two ship's boats and a deal of supplies, and made camp on one of the other islands.'

Most people had already heard this and there had been rumours circulating about why the Commander had not landed here with the rest. There were some murmurings, but Corneliez held up his hand for silence.

'I am sending our new boat to search the islands. The second boat should be ready to launch later today – that will go out to *Batavia*. The first priority is to bring back the remaining water barrels, then what food can be salvaged, then sailcloth to make shelter for us.'

Jan looked about him. At last they would have more water and some shelter. Not before time. They were all parched and rations were running out. Everyone was filthy and there was no privacy; often he would come across some poor soul trying to relieve themselves behind one of the low, scrubby bushes. Many were suffering from the runs and some had infected wounds after their rough journey from the ship.

But they managed a faint cheer as the boat was rowed away from the island and headed northwards.

Corneliez watched the new boat go with a set face. He turned to Jan. 'Keep a lookout for its return, Jan,' he said, 'and come and fetch me as soon as you see it.'

Two hours later, Jan spotted it. He ran to Corneliez, who was surrounded by members of the Council. They were making a list of supplies.

'Good, Jan,' he said, when he heard the news. 'Take the bell and ring it as soon as the boat reaches shore.'

Not long after this, the strange-looking boat came in. Jan rang the bell again and again, as one of the sailors leapt out and pulled her up the sand.

'What news?' asked someone.

The sailor shook his head. 'Both islands are deserted,' he said.

At that moment, Corneliez arrived. 'Deserted?' he repeated.

'Aye, sir. Nothing there but this note, left under a rock on the first island.' He handed it to Corneliez.

All eyes were on Corneliez as he read it. When he had finished, he looked up.

'It is just as I suspected,' he said slowly, 'Your Commander has gone off to save his own skin. He has taken both the ship's boats, a selection of officers and sailors, and a great deal of the ship's food and water.'

'Perhaps he has gone to get help,' said someone nervously.

Corneliez rounded on the speaker. 'The Commander has deserted you!' he shouted.

'He has left us all and looks only to save his own skin. He has taken the ship's boats, so now we have nothing but these two rough vessels.'

Jan bent his head, scared of the rage in the Under Merchant's voice.

'And the Captain, too?' asked someone.

'The Captain is with him,' replied Corneliez. Then he added softly, 'Though I doubt he went of his own free will.'

And Jan again remembered hearing the Captain's harsh voice in the sailors' quarters.

When we make landfall, that's when we'll act.

So we're with the Under Merchant, then. We're with Corneliez!

No, decided Jan, the Captain wouldn't be with the Commander by choice. Jacobsz would have been forced to go with him.

Corneliez raised his voice. 'The Commander has deserted us,' he shouted. 'The Commander is a traitor!'

'Aye, a traitor,' repeated some of the sailors and soldiers. Most of the passengers stayed silent.

'So,' continued Corneliez, 'we now have a name for the island where the note was found.' He waved the note in the air. 'From now on, that island will be known as Traitor's Island.'

Jan was puzzled. Was the Commander really a traitor? He remembered the conversation he'd overheard in the Commander's cabin: *'If the ship cannot be repaired here, we shall have to take the long boat and make for Java.'*

He shrugged. He must have got it wrong. Corneliez was right. The Commander should have been here on the island with all the shipwrecked people. The Commander had deserted them. He was a traitor.

The next days were busy ones for Jan. He was ordered to ring the bell for one announcement after another.

Officers who had failed to command, sailors and soldiers who were previously without any discipline – they all came together under Corneliez as he ordered them back and forth to salvage what cargo they could from *Batavia*. The strange craft built from driftwood were put through their paces, ploughing to and fro, returning laden with barrels and chests, plates and goblets, bayonets, clothes and equipment, and being greeted by Corneliez and members of the Council, who checked the boats' contents and ordered where they should be put.

Batavia's sails were brought to the island, too, and the sailmakers set to work making them into rough tents. Before long, the flat, sparse island was covered with misshapen coverings which gave a little privacy to those who sheltered beneath them.

And all the time, Corneliez was planning with his Council. Sometimes Jan was told to stay close by in case he was needed, and one day he overheard snatches of a conversation between the members.

'This island cannot sustain this great crowd of people, and that's an end to it.'

'But Corneliez, where else can they go?'

'Use your eyes, man! There are plenty more islands.'

'But we don't know if the other islands have water or wildlife. Any people put ashore there might die.'

'They will have as much chance to live there as here.'

There was an uneasy silence, then someone said, 'They could take one of the boats, and then they could return if there was no water.'

'No.' This was Corneliez. 'We keep the boats here. The sailors will row them to the islands and they can go back to check on them from time to time.'

'Aye. Very well.'

Jan moved away out of earshot as the meeting broke up. One of the first to walk away was the preacher. Even though they'd only been shipwrecked for a couple of weeks, he had aged considerably during that time. Always gaunt and pale, now he was nothing but skin and bones, the shreds of his black garments hanging about him forlornly like the feathers of a bedraggled crow.

The preacher glanced up when he saw Jan, but his eyes were distant and he didn't acknowledge him. He muttered to himself as he made his way back to where his family were camped.

'Jan!'

Jan ran to Corneliez.

'Come boy, we have work to do.'

The Under Merchant seemed almost jaunty, his inscrutable face lit, for once, by a smile.

'Sir?'

'Ring that bell and assemble the whole company. I want every man, woman and child to gather round.'

'Aye, sir.'

Jan ran off ringing the bell, visiting each tent in turn.

'Assemble at the shore. The Under Merchant

wishes to make an announcement.'

He was only halfway through his duties when he started to feel faint and dizzy. Although he'd managed to pull out his rotten tooth at last, his mouth still stank with the infection and, like everyone else, he was on strict rations of food and water. He slowed down to get his breath and then, when he had recovered, continued to rouse the others. When he had finished, he made his way slowly to the shore.

Gradually, all who could still walk gathered together to listen.

Corneliez stood with his back to the sea. It was flat calm and the coral beneath the surface was clearly visible through the clear water. He wore a red and gold cloak over his shoulders that contrasted strangely with his stained, loose shirt and torn trousers, but it marked him out from everyone else, as did his intelligent face, his aquiline features and his ice-blue eyes.

Jan stood beside him and continued to ring the bell.

'Enough, cabin boy!' muttered someone from the crowd. 'Stop that racket. We're all here, aren't we?'

Corneliez held up his hand for silence.

'The Council and I have come to some decisions,' he said, smiling down at the crowd. Jan looked up at him and for a moment their eyes met. Jan swallowed nervously.

Corneliez paused, relishing the attention. No one said a word. With a flourish, he took out a scroll. Jan recognised it as a list that Corneliez had been compiling for the last few days, written on paper that had somehow been salvaged from *Batavia*.

'As you can see,' he said, making a sweeping gesture with his hand, 'We are too many for this small island.'

There was some murmuring and anxious glances were exchanged. Corneliez ignored these.

'So,' he continued. 'We must divide ourselves up and some will be taken to the other islands.'

Mutterings broke out. Corneliez held up his hand again.

'First,' he said, 'we are sending a group of soldiers over to High Island – that one over there in the distance' – he gestured vaguely – 'to search for food and water.'

He looked carefully at his list. 'Then,' he continued, 'we shall divide up the remaining survivors between this island and the two nearby.'

He beckoned to Weibbe Hayes, the soldier who had given Jan water, and Weibbe came forward.

'Hayes,' said Corneliez, 'choose two dozen men to take with you to High Island. You will leave in the morning.'

Weibbe looked grim-faced, but he didn't argue. Immediately he set about talking to some of the assembled soldiers.

Corneliez went on. 'And you others – you passengers – you must decide which of you wish to go. You will be taken to Seals' Island and the other nearby island as soon as possible.'

'But what shall we do for victuals? How shall we survive?' asked one of the crowd.

'Those of you sent to other islands will have sufficient food and water to last a week. After that, I shall send someone to check how you fare.' He went on. 'But undoubtedly there is food and water to be had on the other islands, and you will flourish.'

'Will you leave a boat there with us if we go?' asked a tired-looking woman cradling a baby.

'No,' said Corneliez, smoothly. 'The boats will stay here.'

Then, gesturing that no more questions would be answered, Corneliez strode off towards his tent.

The next morning, Weibbe Hayes and his group of some twenty soldiers set off for High Island, to be rowed there by some of the sailors. Jan was sad to see Weibbe leave the island and he went down to the shore to see him off.

Officers helped them load the boats. The sailors who were to escort the group took up their positions and those left behind shoved the vessels into the waves.

Weibbe gave Jan a mock salute. 'When you see smoke rising from High Island, boy,' he said, 'then you'll know we've found food and water.'

Jan nodded. But he couldn't help noticing that they had hardly any provisions on board with them and no weapons. He stared after the boats until they rounded the point and were lost to sight.

The two boats came back to the island later that day, and the next day all the others left. They were mostly passengers – families with children – and a few sailors and servants. They had collected what little they possessed and Corneliez was standing between the two boats as they bobbed up and down in the waves.

Jan watched them crowding on to the boats, enfolding their children and protecting their possessions. The sailors heaved two barrels of water and one of pickled vegetables into each boat.

All those remaining came to see the boats off.

'God speed! We shall pray for you.'

Their shouting went on until the waves drowned out the sound of those in the boats. But the nearer islands weren't far away, and the empty boats had returned by the time the sun was at its highest.

Immediately the boats left, Corneliez called a meeting of the Council, so Jan knew he would not be needed for a while. He walked about the island and watched as the remaining people settled themselves, moving their tents this way and that, spreading themselves. Some women were collecting shellfish and two of the soldiers were walking towards the seal colony with bayonets. Seal meat was keeping the company alive and the trusting animals had still not learnt to avoid the humans who slaughtered them.

He saw the soldier Wouter Looes and stopped to speak to him. As they were speaking, they saw Lucretia come out of her tent and go off on her own.

'Why is she sleeping with the female servants?' asked Jan.

Wouter shrugged. 'She says she feels safer there.'

'But there are no wild animals,' said Jan.

'What should she fear now?'

Wouter looked at Jan. 'There are some beasts that are not animals,' he said quietly, and his eyes slid to the Under Merchant's tent.

Jan frowned. 'Corneliez would not be so dishonourable!' he said angrily, but then he remembered how the Under Merchant had stared after Lucretia.

Wouter didn't answer at once. Then he said. 'Be careful, Jan,' before he turned and walked away.

'What do you mean?' Jan shouted after him. But Wouter went on walking.

More than a week passed, but no boats were sent to check on the people who had been sent to the other islands.

One day, while Jan was doing a job in the Under Merchant's tent, the preacher came to see Corneliez.

'What is it, Preacher?'

The preacher looked awkward, and he adjusted his hat.

'May I be taken to visit the folk on the other islands, Under Merchant? I should like to pray with them for God's protection and His pardon for their sins.'

Corneliez scowled at him. 'Enough of your talk of prayer and sin, Preacher.'

The preacher looked up, shocked. 'But for the sake of their immortal souls, man, they should confess their sins. We must all confess our sins.'

'What is sin, preacher? I don't believe in sin. We have enough troubles on this island, without worrying about such things. And as for those who have left, there's no need to visit them. They will find water and food.'

The preacher looked down at his feet. 'Pray God you are right.'

'There is no fault, no sin. Everything is pre-ordained,' said Corneliez. He turned to Jan. 'Isn't that right, boy?'

Jan had no idea what he meant, but he nodded, not daring to disagree with the Under Merchant when his eyes glittered in such a way.

Chapter Five

A few days later, while Jan was preparing food for Corneliez, he heard raised voices. The Council were meeting and there was clearly some disagreement. Jan stopped plucking the gull he was holding and listened. Corneliez was speaking.

'Caught red-handed, I tell you. The gunner confessed. He has been stealing our wine. Stealing what should be shared equally. He must be punished.'

'Aye, punished perhaps. But not executed!'

Jan stood, rooted to the spot, holding the half-plucked gull. A cold knot of fear gripped his stomach.

'Harsh times, harsh punishment, gentlemen.'
This was Corneliez again.

'And what of the other boy – the other gunner?
He didn't steal the wine. He was merely offered it.'

'He, too, will be executed.'

There was uproar then.

'He's only a boy! He does not deserve this.'

'We cannot agree to this punishment,
Corneliez.'

'Then you are all dismissed,' shouted Corneliez.
'You are no longer my Council. I shall appoint those
who *will* agree.'

Jan edged as far away as he could. He knew that
two young soldiers had been found stealing from
the wine supply. He'd never had much to do with
them, but he knew who they were.

There were more angry voices, and then the
meeting broke up and Corneliez came through to
find him. Jan's hands shook as he plucked again at
the gull's feathers.

Corneliez was smiling. 'When you have served my
food, Jan, I have a job for you.'

For an instant, Jan froze, as Corneliez put a hand
on his shoulder. The Under Merchant, sensing his
fear, spun him round and stared at him.

'Do you remember the disorder on this island, Jan, before I came? The drunkenness and chaos?'

Jan nodded, unable to meet the Under Merchant's gaze.

'And I have brought order to this place, have I not?' His voice was rising.

Jan nodded again.

'So I cannot allow any disobedience.'

'No, sir,' Jan whispered.

'Good lad. Now, when I have eaten, we shall open more of those chests from the ship and I shall choose some clothes to wear. But, meanwhile, I wish to see my new Council.' Then he read Jan a list of names. 'As soon as you have served my meal, Jan, go and fetch these men to me.'

Left alone again, Jan went on with his work, his mind in turmoil. Had Corneliez really just ordered the death of two young soldiers? He had seemed so light-hearted. But he was right. Of course he was right. Any disobedience must be punished. Jan remembered his temptation to steal jewels when they were first shipwrecked, and shuddered. Would he, too, have been executed if he had been discovered?

Later, Jan set off to find the men that Corneliez

had named – the men to be his new Council. Jan couldn't help noticing that many of them had been on the gun deck with Jacobsz that night when Jan had pretended to be asleep.

Aye, we are with the Under Merchant. We are with Corneliez.

The men came as soon as they were called, the new Council convened and, with no dissent, the executions were agreed. They would take place at noon the next day.

During the afternoon, Corneliez called Jan to help him prise open some of the chests from the ship. His tent was large and airy, with salvaged wooden struts to support the canvas and a second tent at the back to store the valuable cargo. It was here that they knelt to unpack some of the fine clothes from the chests.

Jan stared in wonder at the contents. Pieces of ivory, dishes in gold and silver, precious stones, agate ornaments, boots of soft leather, scarlet tunics bright with gold braid, great silver buckles and felt hats with ostrich feathers.

Corneliez strutted about, wearing first this cloak, this ruff, this sword and hat, then others, until he was satisfied.

'There, Jan,' he said at last. 'Now I am the Honourable High Commandant.' He swished the fine red cloak about him. 'And you are my Assistant.'

Jan clapped his hands in pleasure.

He had forgotten that two young men were about to lose their lives.

The next day he was sent to order everyone on the island to attend the execution.

There was a shocked muttering among the crowd as the two boys were led shivering to the shore and forced to kneel.

Jan stared at the ground. He did not want to see who the executioner was and he didn't want to watch the deed, but the screams of the two gunners would echo in his head for hours afterwards.

When the screaming stopped, a dreadful hush descended on the huddled group. Then, at last, the preacher stepped forward and, with some of the officers, removed the bodies for burial on the other side of the island.

Things changed after those first killings.

From that day, no one dared to doubt Corneliez's authority and no one challenged him or his supporters. It was obvious who the supporters were now, for Corneliez gave them fine clothes to wear from the salvaged Company chests and they strutted about the island like so many peacocks.

One day, Corneliez gave Jan special clothes to wear, too, made of fine cloth that didn't scratch his skin, and when Jan stuttered his thanks, he clapped him on the back.

'Well, Jan,' said Corneliez. 'We shall have more of this when we settle in the Indies.'

Jan frowned, puzzled.

Corneliez laughed at him. 'Why boy, my loyal supporters and I are strong, are we not? We have sailors and soldiers and carpenters and cooks among our company, don't we?'

Jan nodded.

'Then we shall overpower any ship that comes to rescue us. We shall sail the seas and one day we shall settle as rich men in the warm islands of the Indies. You are with me, are you not, Jan?'

'Aye, sir, to the death,' said Jan, stumbling over his words, but he couldn't control the shiver that went through him.

'Good boy,' said Corneliez. 'From now on, anyone who is not with me is against me. Anyone who is not with me is a traitor and we must be rid of them.'

Jan nodded. *Of course he is right,* he thought. *Any whiff of disloyalty, any mutterings against him, any criticism of him, must be punished. He is in charge now.*

As time went on, there were more executions. Nearly every day someone was accused of disloyalty to the Under Merchant and killed. Men – and women too – were hacked to death or drowned. The soldiers were the worst murderers. They showed no mercy and hunted down their victims, sometimes only because of a glance or an imagined slight.

Once, when Jan was coming back to Corneliez's tent, he saw one of the young deck hands blindfolded, kneeling on the ground in front of the Under Merchant, his head bowed. One of the soldiers handed Corneliez a bayonet which he'd just sharpened.

Corneliez glanced up as Jan approached.

'How loyal are you to me, Jan?' he asked, fingering the bayonet.

Jan started to tremble. He couldn't look at

the kneeling boy. 'To the death, sir,' he muttered automatically.

Corneliez thrust the bayonet into Jan's hands. 'Then test this weapon's sharpness on that traitor's neck,' he whispered, pointing at the young deck-hand.

Still trembling, Jan took the bayonet. It was so heavy! He swallowed and tried to stop his hands shaking. He must obey. He *would* do it, he *would* show himself to be a man. He forced himself to hold the bayonet steady and walked forwards.

But then Corneliez laughed, and beckoned the soldier to come over. 'The cabin boy's not used to using weapons. You test its sharpness, soldier,' he said, taking the bayonet from Jan. The soldier needed no urging and ran towards the kneeling boy, the bayonet's blade glinting in the sun, and in no time the deed was done and the soldier was wiping the blade clean.

Jan sank to his knees and burst into tears. 'I would have done it for you, sir,' he shouted, between sobs, holding on to the folds of Corneliez's red cloak. 'I was ready to do it.'

Corneliez pushed him away. 'You'll have another chance, boy,' he said curtly. Then he turned to the soldier, laughing. 'Take the body away.'

That day, another ruling was made. Corneliez sent Jan round to the remaining passengers.

'All young women are to be under the protection of one of the Council members,' announced Jan to every family.

'What does this mean?' whispered the mother of a fifteen-year-old girl.

Jan knew very well what it meant, and he looked boldly at the girl. 'It means that your daughter must go to live with one of the Council members so that she is better protected. It is the Under Merchant's decree,' he said, suddenly wishing that he, too, was a member of the Council.

The girl looked despairingly at her mother, who wept silently as Jan left.

When Jan went back to tell Corneliez that he had made the announcement, Corneliez put his arm round Jan's shoulders. 'And you, too, Jan,' he said. 'You can take one of the women to be with you. It is time you became a man.'

Jan blushed. No woman had ever looked at him twice. But there was someone he wanted. He wanted the beautiful daughter of the preacher. She was called Judith, and he'd often watched her as she walked with her father or played with her younger brothers and sisters. But she'd only ever looked at him with disgust. Well, she wouldn't be able to do that now. If he chose her, she would have to obey. It was the Under Merchant's decree. And everyone knew what happened now if you went against *that*.

'Well, Jan, who is it to be?'

'Judith, sir,' said Jan. 'The preacher's daughter, Judith.'

Corneliez laughed. 'No, Jan, I'm afraid you are too late. She is already taken by one of the Council members. You'll have to look elsewhere.'

Jan knew better than to get on the wrong side of a Council member. There were plenty of other women – and none of them would dare resist him now that he had the ear of the Under Merchant – but there were none so fair as Judith. Even the pretty fifteen-year-old wasn't as lovely as Judith.

Jan knew who Corneliez had chosen. A few days earlier he had seen the Under Merchant speaking to Lucretia and had overheard snatches of their conversation.

'I can protect you, Lucretia. Come and stay with me.'

She had replied steadily, 'You know I have a husband waiting for me in Java.'

'Java!' Corneliez had laughed. 'You will never see Java now.'

She had said nothing, and Corneliez had gone close to her and started to play with her hair. It had begun to grow back after its brutal hacking on board *Batavia*.

'You know that I cannot protect you if you do not do as I say, Lucretia,' he whispered. There was a pause. 'Those who are not with me, are against me.'

Lucretia had stared coldly into his eyes. 'Very well,' she said at last.

But she had not wanted this, Jan knew it. She had simply chosen to live rather than to die. Even Wouter Looes would not have been able to help her if she had refused the Under Merchant.

It was Wouter Looes who brought the news to Corneliez.

'Smoke, sir! Smoke on High Island.'

Jan looked up from chopping seal meat. What had Wiebbe Hayes said as he left? *'When you see smoke rising from High island. Then you'll know we've found food and water.'*

Jan's heart leapt, but he kept his head down and went on chopping. Weibbe was alive. And not only alive, but they had found food and water!

But Corneliez was furious. He strode down to the shore to look across to the distant island. There was no doubt about it: a thin column of smoke was rising from the island into the blue sky.

Seeing the Under Merchant's fury, no one dared to cheer, though many were secretly heartened.

'It is a trick!' yelled Corneliez. 'They are traitors and they are pretending they have found food and water. That is what this means.' He wiped the spittle from around his lips with his red and gold cloak and continued, 'They will lure us to the island and then they will kill us.'

'Surely not,' muttered the preacher, but his wife silenced him.

'Well, we'll play them at their own game,' shouted Corneliez. 'We shall gather our troops and attack *them.*'

He turned once more to look at the smoke

and then spat on the ground.

'And we'll root out all the other traitors, too,' he cried. 'Those on Seals' Island and the other island. They were all against me. They are all traitors.'

Wouter Looes was standing near Jan. 'They won't have survived, those others,' he said quietly. 'The Under Merchant knew there was no water on those islands.'

Jan said nothing. He did not know what to think.

The next day there was more bad news for Corneliez, and no one wanted to break it to him – one of the soldiers told Jan instead.

'Some of the sailors and a couple of carpenters have taken the boat they built. They got away last night under cover of darkness, and we think they've gone to High Island to join Weibbe. You tell the Under Merchant, Jan. You are his favourite. It will be better coming from you.'

Jan's hands shook as he relayed the message to Corneliez but, to his surprise, Corneliez remained calm. He smiled grimly.

'Then I was right, Jan. It proves I was right. More traitors have gone to join the others. We shall seek them out and destroy them.' He gathered his cloak about him and strode out of his tent, and as he did so, he shouted, 'But first we shall have a game with those others nearer to us, eh, Jan?'

'Sir?' said Jan.

'Why, all those wretches on Seals' Island and the other island who fled from here.'

Jan frowned. Surely Corneliez had *sent* them to the near islands, hadn't he? But perhaps he had misunderstood. Perhaps those people all went because they were not loyal to the Under Merchant.

Jan had little time to reflect on this, because later that day he found himself armed with a dagger and loaded into the remaining boat with a group of soldiers. As the sailors rowed them away from shore, Jan looked back, Corneliez's instructions ringing in his ears.

'I want none of those wretches left alive, do you understand?'

Some of the soldiers had grinned, feeling the blades of their bayonets with their calloused thumbs.

'Aye, sir!'

Corneliez had given them all generous portions

of wine before they left and there was much lewd talk and laughter among the men.

'They won't give much resistance,' said one.

'Lambs to the slaughter,' said another.

Jan wasn't used to wine and it had gone to his head. The Under Merchant had given him special instructions:

'I expect you to kill one of those traitors for me Jan,' he had said, clapping him on the back. 'You are a grown man now, so it's time you proved yourself.'

As the boat skimmed over the shallow waters above the coral and then into the sea beyond, Jan felt proud. He was a man now, and the Under Merchant's trusted Assistant. No, not Under Merchant – he mustn't forget that Corneliez liked Jan to address him as High Commandant now. He was Assistant to the High Commandant.

The soldiers leapt ashore as the boat grounded, leaving the sailors to pull it up on to the beach. Shouting and swinging their bayonets round their heads, they ran this way and that.

As Wouter had predicted, there were hardly any people left alive and the survivors were in no state to put up a fight. Roaring and whooping, the soldiers struck down any soul who showed a sign of life.

Jan looked around desperately. The soldiers were doing it all. There would be no one left for him to kill.

And then, out of the corner of his eye, he saw a tiny movement behind a bush. It could have been a bird – or it *could* be another of the traitors. His head still fuddled with wine, Jan tried to focus. The soldiers had overtaken him by now and gone ahead, making a systematic search of the island.

If this was another traitor, they had missed him – or her. Even in his drunken state, Jan hoped it was not a woman. Whoever it was, would be weakened by thirst and starvation, for there was even less vegetation on this barren island than on the one they had just come from. Jan ran towards the bush, the wine giving him courage.

But when he reached the place, he hesitated. Nothing moved. Maybe there was no one there. Maybe it had just been the flutter of a seabird.

He walked forward cautiously, his dagger clutched in his hand, and peered behind the bush.

Then he jumped back. There *was* someone there! And it was someone he recognised – but only just. It was one of his fellow cabin boys from *Batavia*. Now the lad was nothing but skin and bone, his exposed flesh blistered and his eyes closed. But he was still breathing.

Jan closed his mind to everything but the command he'd been given. He raised his dagger.

The boy moaned and tried to open his eyes.

Jan hesitated. Then suddenly he remembered that this boy had been one of those who'd taunted him for his pockmarked skin and stinking breath.

With an angry strength, Jan drove his dagger into the boy's chest.

There was a ghastly noise. Not so much a scream – for the boy's throat was so parched that he couldn't scream; rather a convulsive gurgle. Just for a moment he looked at Jan, then his head lolled on to the ground, his body twitched and was still.

Jan pulled out the dagger and plunged it in the ground to clean it. He turned and ran back to the shore. Then he vomited into the waves.

Well, he was a man now. He had killed for Corneliez. It was easy. He could kill again.

Back on their own island, the landing party reported to Corneliez that every person on Seals' Island was now dead from lack of food and water, or had been murdered.

'Every one?'

Jan looked at the soldiers and wondered whether they would tell Corneliez what they'd learnt. Apparently, one of the men on Seals' Island, the one who had put up most resistance, had yelled at them as they struck him down: 'You won't kill us all, you murderers. Some of us have escaped to be with Hayes and his men.'

Jan watched as the soldiers glanced at one another.

'Every one?' repeated Corneliez.

'It seems that a few have escaped from the island. They made a boat from driftwood,' said a Lance Corporal.

'Pah!' spat Corneliez. 'They won't have got far. They will have drowned.'

Corneliez was full of praise for Jan when he heard about the cabin boy.

'Now you are bloodied, Jan,' said Corneliez, giving him a goblet of wine. "Now you are indeed my man – my Chief Assistant.'

Jan looked at his feet. He couldn't forget the look in the cabin boy's eyes as the dagger struck him.

But when he had gulped down the wine, he felt braver. Brave enough to run round the island threatening to kill anyone who annoyed him. And brave enough to go and seek out that young girl he had seen with her mother when he had gone to tell them of the Under Merchant's plans for unprotected women and girls.

He lurched into their tent, his dagger drawn, and looked about him.

There was no sign of the girl. 'Where is she?' he shouted at her mother, slurring his words. 'I want your daughter – where is she?'

The mother slowly rose to her feet, her eyes on Jan's dagger.

'She is not here,' she said quietly.

'I can see that,' yelled Jan. 'Where is she?'

The woman looked straight into Jan's eyes.

'Take me, boy,' she said, her voice steady, though her whole body trembled. 'I can quench your passion.'

For a moment Jan was speechless. He stared at the woman through blurred eyes. Although she was not as pretty as her daughter, she was not that old, and she was good-looking.

She came up to him and stroked his face.

Jan didn't see the disgust in her eyes. He was conscious of her body close to his and of the shape of her breasts under her tattered dress.

His grip loosened on the dagger and it fell to the ground.

Chapter Six

The only people left now were either with Jan and the others on one island, or with Wiebbe Hayes on High Island.

The remaining passengers were cowed and terrified. They dared say nothing to Corneliez or his supporters so they kept silent. And they looked at Jan differently, with eyes full of fear. No one mocked him now.

Jan closed his ears and his eyes to much of what went on around him. People disappeared. A sick boy was murdered one night – he'd overheard Corneliez order the killing. And a baby had been strangled for crying and disturbing the Under Merchant's sleep. Sometimes, as he watched the Under Merchant,

Jan wondered that he could be in such good spirits after each killing. Yet he himself never did any killing.

Jan knew that he must never show any sign of weakening; he'd seen what happened to others who faltered in their loyalty. Often Corneliez said to him, 'We must be strong, Jan. Our band must be strong. We must get rid of the weak ones.'

Jan still lusted after the preacher's daughter, Judith, but she was now beyond his reach. She had moved into the tent of one of the Council members and he appeared to treat her well.

But the preacher himself was a broken man. Jan observed him as he shuffled round the island with his holy books, muttering prayers.

Jan would sometimes go to the preacher's tent and play with the baby boy. Although the toddler always welcomed Jan and stretched out his arms to him, the rest of the family looked at him with suspicion. But at least the older children didn't taunt him, as they had in the past. They were too afraid.

'Our preacher is a sad sight, is he not?' said Corneliez one day, as he observed the man walking away from the tents, his head bowed.

'Aye, sir,' said Jan.

Corneliez smiled. He seemed amused by the powerlessness of this once-influential man.

'We'll cheer him up, then, shall we Jan?' he said. 'We'll invite him to dine with us tonight.'

Jan looked up. 'Shall I go and tell him?'

'Yes, Jan. Tell him to come, and we'll get that lovely daughter of his here, too.'

The preacher looked horrified when Jan told him that he and Judith were summoned to eat with Corneliez, but he could not refuse.

'Am I to bring my wife, too?'

'No,' said Jan. He says just you and your eldest daughter.'

For the rest of the day, Jan was kept busy preparing what food he could muster for the evening meal. Corneliez and the Council members had the best of what was left of the stores from *Batavia*, but there was little enough and Jan had to cook seal meat to go with the salt pork and pickled vegetables.

When the preacher and Judith arrived, Corneliez was in high spirits. He opened a new barrel of wine and told Jan to offer it to the guests.

'No, no,' said the preacher, waving his hand and dismissing Jan, but Corneliez, still smiling, said. 'Give the preacher wine, Jan.' He paused. 'And see that he drinks it.'

The preacher was about to protest again, but Judith looked over at him and shook her head. Jan filled the goblet.

'Drink, Preacher!' said Corneliez, and the preacher nervously raised the goblet to his lips.

'Drain it, man!' said Corneliez. The preacher obeyed, though Jan could see that he was hardly able to swallow.

'Refill the preacher's goblet, Jan,' said Corneliez.

Judith looked over at her father and then at Corneliez. 'Please,' she said quietly. 'Let him be.'

'Nonsense, girl,' said Corneliez. 'Wine will improve his spirits.'

Again and again Jan was instructed to refill the preacher's goblet. And again and again Corneliez forced him to drain it. It was only when the man was almost insensible that Corneliez seemed to tire of this amusement.

When the meal was nearly over, Jan went outside to sluice down some dishes in sea water and as he stood there, wiping the plates, thinking of Judith and wishing she could have been his, his reverie was shattered.

A terrible scream came from the tent of the preacher's family. Jan froze, hugging a dish to his chest. There was another scream, and another and another, followed by the sound of men thumping and grunting. Then a horrible silence, worse even than the screaming.

Jan continued to stand rooted to the spot, until he saw a party of soldiers emerging from the preacher's tent – a party that included Wouter Looes. It was only then that he forced himself to go back inside the Under Merchant's tent.

The preacher had heard nothing; he was slumped unconscious on the ground. But Judith had certainly heard, and she sat by her father's side, her hands held over her ears, moaning and rocking to and fro.

Later that evening, when the preacher had staggered away and Judith had been taken back to the tent of her protector, Wouter Looes came to report to Corneliez.

'Are they all dead, Wouter?'

'Aye, sir. Every one.'

Jan couldn't sleep that night. He kept imagining the preacher when he finally reached his tent and discovered that his family had been slaughtered while he was at table with the Under Merchant.

He thought that nothing more could shock him until the next day he saw Judith, white-faced and sobbing, clinging to her father, who seemed to have become an old man overnight.

Jan went looking for Wouter, and when he found him, he asked, 'Was the baby boy killed, too?'

Wouter nodded. 'Skull smashed,' he said gruffly. He wouldn't meet Jan's eye.

Jan turned away, remembering the happy little boy who had smiled at him on *Batavia*. Then he straightened his shoulders. Corneliez was their leader. He knew what he was doing. He had told Jan that they had to get rid of any who were weak, any who would be a drain on their diminishing resources. His words still echoed in Jan's head. 'You wait, Jan,' he'd said. 'My loyal band and I will have a high time when we are away from here and living in the Indies.'

'A high time,' repeated Jan to himself. And he tried to forget the face of that smiling child.

Meanwhile, the smoke on High Island continued to rise and taunt Corneliez, and his fury mounted.

When he could stand it no longer, he appointed one of his councillors to lead an attack on High Island. So a few days later, when all the weapons had been gathered and prepared, a group of soldiers set off.

Corneliez did not go with them but stayed back at base, pacing up and down the shore. Jan was beside him.

'We shall defeat the traitors, Jan, then everyone on these islands will be loyal to me. I shall force them to sign an oath.'

Jan shaded his eyes and looked towards High Island, but it was too far away to detect any movement. All he could see was the smoke still rising from the fires there.

For a moment, Jan remembered the kindness shown to him by Wiebbe Hayes, but he quickly put the memory out of his head. Corneliez had told everyone that Wiebbe was a traitor. And Jan was Corneliez's loyal follower, his Assistant. He had killed for him – not just the cabin boy on Seals' Island: he had helped kill two others as well. And he would kill again, whenever he was asked.

All day they waited for the boats to return. It was early evening before the first of them rounded the point and, as soon as they were in sight, Corneliez waded out into the water. Jan watched him.

'What news? Are they defeated?' shouted Corneliez.

'Sir, they are armed!' said the first man out of the boat. 'Weibbe Hayes has armed his men.'

'Armed?' shouted Corneliez. 'What with, man? They had no weapons when they left.'

'They have now,' said the man. 'They have catapults and pikes and other weapons they have made from driftwood and barrel hoop-iron. We could not overcome them. They are too strong. They are well-fed and healthy. There are wild beasts and mutton birds on the island, and plenty of water.'

Corneliez's face twisted with rage.

'Could you not defeat Hayes and a handful of soldiers? And you call yourselves men?'

'There are over forty men with Hayes,' said a Lance Corporal.

'Forty!' exploded Corneliez. 'But he left with only twenty-four.'

'Aye, but many have joined him – from Seals' Island – and the carpenters and sailors from here.'

'Traitors!' spat out Corneliez.

'What would you have us do now?' asked the Lance Corporal. 'Shall we try again?'

'Let me think on it,' said Corneliez, and he turned and walked back to his tent.

A week later, they tried again, and this time Corneliez went with them, watching from a boat on the water. But again, they were repelled by Hayes.

During the next few weeks, Corneliez was in a vile mood. His temper was becoming increasingly short and Jan kept out of his way, serving him as unobtrusively as he could and never speaking unless spoken to.

Then one day Corneliez's temper improved. He slapped Jan on the shoulders.

'Today, Jan, each man shall sign an oath of allegience to me. Go and round them up and bring them here to my tent. Every one of them, mind.'

Although they grumbled, no one dared disobey. Even the preacher signed the oath. Jan watched as his pen wavered over the piece of parchment, and saw him glance in the direction of the tent where Judith stayed as, finally, he put his name to the document.

After the preacher had signed, Corneliez took him aside. Jan had been throwing sand on each signature to dry it, and he overheard their conversation.

'It is good that you have sworn loyalty to me, Preacher, for I have a special job for you,' he said.

Jan looked up and saw the preacher's drained, anxious face as Corneliez went on. 'You, of all the men here, are the one whom those traitors will trust, so tomorrow you shall go to High Island to negotiate peace with Hayes and his men.'

'Peace?' whispered the preacher, a flicker of hope in his eyes.

'Aye,' said Corneliez. 'Peace.' And he walked off, smiling. Then he turned and spoke quietly to Jan. 'You shall go with him, Jan. You shall be my eyes and ears.'

Jan didn't want to go, but he was proud to be trusted by the Under Merchant.

Later that day, when Jan was looking for shellfish to cook, he saw the preacher at his prayers on the far side of the island, tears running down his pale cheeks. Again Jan remembered the little boy. He turned away and went to another part of the island.

The next day, a boatload of soldiers and sailors rowed Jan and the preacher to High Island.

Jan was expecting to stay in the boat, but the preacher asked him to go with him. Nervously, they walked together up from the beach.

'No wonder Hayes and his men have survived here,' said the preacher, looking about him as they headed inland.

Jan nodded. The terrain here looked different. There were rocks and much more vegetation.

They were hardly out of sight of the boat when they heard someone call, 'Are you alone, Preacher?'

It was Hayes!

The preacher cleared his throat. 'I have Jan Pelgrom with me.' He paused. 'Jan Pelgrom the cabin boy.'

Jan's mouth was dry and his legs would not obey him. He could see that the preacher, too, was shaking. At last, Wiebbe showed himself and waited for them, leaning against a rock. Behind him, Jan noticed a roughly constructed wall offering protection from attack. They were clearly organised, these men of Wiebbe's.

'Don't be afraid, man,' said Wiebbe to the preacher, as they drew closer. 'I know that you are no murderer.'

At first, the preacher was too scared to do

anything except shake his head, but at last he found his voice.

'I have been sent to negotiate peace with you and your men, Wiebbe,' he said.

'On what terms?'

'Corneliez has offered to bring wine and blankets for you and your soldiers in exchange for your boat.'

For a long time Wiebbe didn't reply. Then, at last, he spoke again and, as he did, he looked at Jan and smiled. Jan had missed that smile!

'Very well. Tell the Under Merchant that I will meet him on the shore tomorrow. He is to bring the promised goods himself and in exchange, I shall let him take our boat. ' He smiled. 'We have plenty of carpenters here to make another.'

Then he looked at Jan. 'Did you look out for the smoke rising from our island, Jan, as I said?'

Jan looked up and met his eyes. 'Aye, Wiebbe,' he said. 'And I was glad for you.'

Wiebbe put his hand briefly on Jan's arm, then turned and strode away. Jan felt tears coming to his eyes, but he wiped them away angrily. He must remember that Weibbe was a traitor!

Relieved to have delivered the message and still

frightened that they would be attacked, Jan and the preacher made their way quickly back to the boat over the uneven ground.

When they reported back to Corneliez, he received the information thoughtfully. To the preacher he said, 'Well done, man. Now we shall have some peace.'

But later, he gathered some of the soldiers to his tent and Jan heard him giving them instructions.

'As soon as I land with the goods tomorrow, attack again. They won't be expecting it. We shall have them this time,' he said, and he rubbed his hands together until the knuckles cracked.

The next day, Jan watched as the boats were loaded with wine and blankets before they set off again for High Island. This time, Corneliez was on board and Jan was left behind.

'Only fighting men this time,' said Corneliz curtly, when Jan begged to go too.

All day Jan paced up and down the shoreline waiting for the boats to return but when, at last, they came into view and those left on the island shouted at the sailors and soldiers for news, there were no answering shouts. The men simply rowed on in grim silence.

The silence made Jan nervous. He stared at the boats looking for Corneliez, but there was no sign of him.

He waded out into the water as far as he dared. 'Where is the Under Merchant?' he yelled, as the boats came in closer. But his words were snatched away by the wind.

The people on the shore crowded round the returning sailors and soldiers, and Jan found himself shoved out of the way.

'What news? Is Weibbe defeated?'

Jan didn't hear the answer, but he did hear a shout of disbelief from the man standing next to him.

'Captured! Captured, you say? Who is captured?'

'Corneliez.'

Everyone spoke at once, and the crowd surged forward to hear more.

'Quiet!' It was one of the Council members. 'Let us hear what happened.' He pointed to one of the sailors. 'You, man. Tell us.'

The sailor had a gruff voice. 'We were fools,' he said. 'We should have known Wiebbe for the slippery eel he is.'

'What happened?'

The sailor cleared his throat. 'Weibbe must have suspected something,' he said. 'As soon as Corneliez and his party landed, Wiebbe's men rushed at them.'

'Didn't you fire from the boat?' asked someone.

The sailor nodded. 'Our covering fire caught some of Weibbe's men, but not before Corneliez was overpowered and taken prisoner.'

Another soldier continued, 'As soon as we saw what was happening, we went ashore, but we were driven back. Wiebbe's men were too strong for us.'

Jan felt as though a knife had been turned in his innards. The Under Merchant captured! What would happen to them now? Without the Under Merchant they were nothing.

Now there was no one to cook for, wash and clean for, and strike the ship's bell for.

He wandered around in a daze.

A little way off he saw a group of soldiers talking urgently outside one of the tents. After a while, they went their separate ways. Wouter Looes headed towards Jan.

'What are you going to do, Wouter?' asked Jan.

Wouter looked at Jan. 'We must attack Hayes again and rescue the Under Merchant,' he said. 'The others have put me in charge.' Then, as he was walking away, he stopped briefly and turned back. 'We can do nothing without Corneliez,' he said. 'We must have leadership.'

Later that night there was a commotion in one of the womens' tents. It seemed that, as soon as Lucretia had heard of Corneliez's capture, she had left his tent and gone to sleep with some of the other women who had not been selected by members of the Council. Now some of the soldiers had come looking for her, intent on forcing themselves on her.

But they had reckoned without Wouter. Jan heard his voice raised in anger. 'I am your leader now!' he yelled. 'You have elected me, and I give the orders. Leave the lady alone! That is my order, and anyone who disobeys it will feel my dagger in their heart.'

There was a sullenness now among the mutineers, and the atmosphere was worse than ever. There was not much left of the food salvaged from *Batavia,* but they had all learnt to gather what little the island afforded and to preserve the rainwater. Even so, many had sores and infections, and blisters from exposure to sun and wind.

The soldiers talked of having seen leaping, furry creatures on High Island with huge back legs, tiny front legs and doe-like eyes. These, and the big birds that nested nearby, had clearly provided Hayes and his men with a good supply of meat – and Hayes had sunk wells on the island so water was plentiful too. It was no wonder that they were stronger.

These were compelling reasons for defeating Weibbe and his men. Everyone was desperate, not only for vengeance, but also for good food and fresh water.

Two weeks after Corneliez's capture by Wiebbe, Wouter was ready to attack, and once again, the boats set off for High Island. This time, Jan was pressed into action.

'Make yourself useful, Jan,' Wouter said. 'You say you enjoy killing. Let's see what you are made of.'

Reluctantly, Jan climbed into one of the boats. His lust for blood wasn't as strong now and he didn't feel brave at all without the Under Merchant's protection. The soldiers with him were working themselves into a frenzy – boasting of what they would do to those they captured.

Jan joined in their talk, but he knew he was no match for a fighting man. He might have killed a half-dead cabin boy and he had helped kill a couple of other passengers, but he was a weakling. Wiebbe Hayes's men were sure to be well-disciplined, and Jan would be cut down in an instant. The soldiers in the boat had muskets and sharpened bayonets, but Jan was only given a dagger with which to defend himself.

'No good wasting good weapons on you, boy,' joked one of the soldiers, drawing a horny hand across the sharp blade of his bayonet.

As they drew closer to High Island, Jan could hear his heart pounding and feel the blood singing in his ears.

At last they rounded the point, the island came into view and the sailors guided the home-made craft through the breaking waves and on to the shore.

Wouter went round each group in turn.

'You have your orders,' he said quietly. 'See that you carry them out. If you kill traitors, so much the better, but we must rescue Corneliez.'

'Look behind you, Wouter,' said one of the soldiers, pointing. They all looked – and Jan tried to swallow, but his mouth was dry. On the dunes above them, Wiebbe's men had appeared and were lined up, ready. There were no muskets or bayonets to be seen, but they were armed with homemade clubs and slings and pikes.

'We knew they'd be expecting us,' said Wouter fiercely. 'Just remember what we agreed.'

'Aye', said the men with one voice. Then Wouter shouted orders and Corneliez's followers swarmed up the beach, some swinging bayonets round their heads and others firing muskets.

Jan ran with them, but all at once he stumbled and tripped, and by the time he had righted himself he was behind the rest. Weibbe's men might be stronger, but Wouter and the others were desperate. This was their last chance. Without Corneliez they would not survive. Without food and water they would not survive.

Jan tried to run forward to join the others. He must not be branded a coward! But when he put weight on his ankle, he realised that he could hardly walk, let alone fight.

Desperately he looked about him. The fighting

above and beyond him was fierce. There were screams and shouts and gunfire. As he listened, the noise grew more distant. What did that mean? Had Wouter and the others gained ground?

Miserably, he limped a little way towards the sound of the battle, but every step was agony. Furious with himself, he retraced his steps, hoping to huddle out of sight beside one of the boats. But no – the sailors with the boats had rowed a little way out to keep them safe from Wiebbe's men.

Jan sat in the shade of a rock at the water's edge trembling with fear. What would Wouter and his men do to him when they returned? He would be branded a coward.

He sat there for what seemed like hours, straining his ears. Occasionally he heard the sound of fighting, but it was far away now.

And then he heard a noise much nearer. Clasping his dagger, he tried to flatten himself against the rock.

Two men were running down the shore, keeping low and dodging between the dunes. They were running straight for him. They couldn't avoid seeing him and he could do nothing to defend himself.

He closed his eyes, waiting for the blow. Then they were upon him.

'Ye gods,' said one. 'Who's this?'

Fearfully, Jan opened his eyes and looked up.

It was Weibbe! Wiebbe with one of his soldiers.

The soldier raised the club in his hand, but Wiebbe stopped him.

'No. Not yet, soldier. I know this lad.'

Wiebbe crouched down beside him. 'Oh, Jan,' he said. 'What have they made you do, boy? What has Corneliez turned you into?'

Slowly, still trembling, Jan raised his eyes and looked up at Wiebbe's grizzled face. As he stared at him he remembered all the small kindnesses Wiebbe had shown him on board, speaking to him when others ignored him, offering him the last of his water when Jan was desperate with thirst.

Jan felt a sob rising in his throat. As he looked into Weibbe's eyes, he began to realise the horror of what he had done. The terror and confusion of the last weeks welled up in him and he clung to Wiebbe, choking and heaving.

'Jan, Jan,' sighed Weibbe again, shaking his head.

Then he turned to the soldier. 'Give me your

club and leave us for a moment.'

'But Wiebbe, the ship! We must warn them!'

'Only a moment, I promise you.'

Then Wiebbe said to Jan. 'Ask God to forgive you your sins, Jan.'

'Are you going to kill me?' sobbed Jan.

Wiebbe shook his head. 'No, I'm going to tell you something, Jan. We have sighted the Company's rescue ship, the *Sardam,* and we're going to row out to warn those on board what is happening on these islands.'

He pulled Jan to his feet and pointed. 'Look, boy. Look over there.'

Jan rubbed the tears from his eyes and stared at the ship clearly visible a little way off.

'Wiebbe, we must go!' said his companion. 'The ship has been sighted by others, too. The Under Merchant's followers will row out to the *Sardam.* We must get there first and warn Pelsaert.'

'Aye. I'm coming.' Then Wiebbe turned to Jan. 'This is the last favour I shall do for you, boy.'

And saying that, he swung the club down on to Jan's head. It was not hard enough to crush his skull, but strong enough to render him senseless. He fell to the ground.

For a moment Wiebbe stood over him. 'When they find him, they'll think he was in the fight. At least those barbarians won't brand him a coward.'

Then he and his companion ran on, round the next point to where their homemade boat was hidden.

Chapter Seven

Jan remembered little of what happened next. He drifted in and out of consciousness, unaware of the drama unfolding around him.

Someone lifted him into a boat. Later, he woke up lying under canvas. His befuddled mind couldn't understand where he was. Feebly, he tried to sit up, but his head was hammering with pain and he closed his eyes again.

The next time he awoke some hours later, his mind was clearer, though his head still throbbed.

He sat up and looked around him. It was then he noticed that his legs were shackled and that he was not alone. He was surrounded by faces he knew only too well – the faces of Corneliez's supporters.

He leaned over, clutching his head between his hands.

'Where are we?' he muttered.

One of the soldiers spat. 'We're under guard on Seals' Island. We're done for, Jan. That damned Commander has returned.'

'Pelsaert?'

'Aye, Pelsaert. He reached Java and has returned on a Company ship manned with soldiers and Company officials.'

Another voice drifted to Jan through his pain. 'Hayes sighted the ship and rowed out to warn him. Then Pelsaert sent his troops to round us up. We didn't stand a chance. The Company soldiers were armed to the teeth.'

Vaguely now, Jan remembered Weibbe's face in front of his own, his arms underneath Jan's shoulders, forcing him up to look out at the *Sardam*.

'Where is Corneliez?' he asked. 'Is he alive? And has the Captain been brought back here with Pelsaert?'

'The Under Merchant's alive, all right. He's being questioned by the Commander. But as for the Captain, no one knows his fate. Pelsaert left him in Java. He won't be working for the Company again, that's for certain.'

'And the preacher – and the lady – what of them?'

'They are on board the *Sardam.*'

Jan felt dizzy and sick. He tried to swallow, but his mouth was too dry.

'What will happen to us?' he whispered.

There was a heavy silence, then a voice he recognised. It was Wouter.

'Expect no mercy, Jan. We are mutineers – and you know what happens to mutineers.'

Jan lay down again. He turned his face away and sobbed silently into his filthy shirt. Yes – he knew only too well what happened to mutineers.

Pelsaert was a thorough man. Every one of the mutineers was questioned and tried. Day after day the soldiers and sailors were taken, one by one, to be tried at a makeshift court on Seals' Island. Corneliez, still arrogant, had boasted of his loyal band of pirates and named them all, so there was little point in denying their guilt – though some did, and only confessed to their crimes under torture.

Corneliez was the first to be sentenced: to be hanged on Seals' Island.

Day after day the verdicts were read out:

'To be hanged on Seals' Island.'

'To be taken back to Java and his guilt investigated further.'

'To be hanged on Seals' Island.'

'To be whipped.'

'To be keel-hauled.'

'To be hanged on Seals' Island.'

One by one the mutineers were sentenced. Jan waited his turn with the others. Wouter returned just before Jan was taken to see Pelsaert.

'What news, Wouter?' he asked.

Wouter shook his head. 'The Commander hasn't given me a sentence. He said he would give it more consideration.'

'Why?'

Wouter shrugged. 'He heard that I tried to protect Lucretia van der Meylen.'

'Perhaps you will be pardoned.'

Wouter gave a mirthless laugh. 'No, Jan. That will never happen.'

Jan he knew he could expect no mercy. He had been the Under Merchant's right hand man, he had killed a cabin boy, he had assisted at the killing of women passengers, and he had forced himself on married women.

When it was his turn he shuffled forward, his head lowered. His crimes were read out and, trying to hold back the tears, he confessed to them.

'How old are you, Jan Pelgrom?' asked Pelsaert.

'Eighteen, sir.'

Pelsaert looked up. 'Only a boy,' he muttered.

Then he wrote something down.

'Dismissed,' he said. 'To be hanged on Seals' Island on October the second.'

October the second. Pelsaert had been thorough but quick. The date for the hangings was fixed only two weeks after the last battle between Weibbe Hayes and the mutineers.

Jan heard the ship's carpenters at work making the scaffolds.

Only a few days left on this earth. He tried to pray, to ask for forgiveness for his crimes, for he feared hell even more than he feared the noose of the hangman. But how could God forgive him for what he had done? He had killed innocent people and forced himself on women. It had seemed right when he had been under the protection of the Under Merchant, when he had revelled in his reflected power, when the killing had been some sort of gruesome game. But Corneliez could protect no one now. He was gone, chained in the bowels of the *Sardam.*

And then the fateful day dawned.

The whole ship's company of the *Sardam* and all the mutineers were assembled on Seals' Island. The preacher was there, too, to say prayers with those who were to die. But all the remaining passengers, including Lucretia, stayed on board the *Sardam.* They had seen too much death already.

Jan looked up at the gibbets, ready for their human loads, and at first he was numb. But then, when the names were read out, he started to tremble. He wanted to be brave, but his body let him down and he felt warm liquid spreading in his trousers.

Corneliez went first. Jan forced himself to look at the man whom he had followed without question, the man who had made him feel important and who had made him think that to realise their dream of wealth and comfort, they had to kill everyone in their way.

The preacher started to pray, but the Under Merchant cut him short. He fought to the last, screaming and protesting, but finally he was silenced, and Jan shuddered as he watched Corneliez's body twitching beneath the rope and heard him choking.

He didn't look at the others. He waited his turn, shaking, with his head bowed.

'Jan Pelgrom de Bye!'

As his name was called, he was pushed forward by one of the soldiers from the *Sardam*.

He looked up then – and caught the eye of Pelsaert, who had been watching impassively as each mutineer was hanged.

All at once, Jan struggled from the grip of the soldier who held him and flung himself at Pelsaert's feet.

'Please sir, I am too young. Please don't let me die. I had to do what I did. The Under Merchant forced me and I had to obey him. Please!'

By now, the soldier had caught hold of him again. 'Come on, boy,' he said gruffly.

But Pelsaert held up his hand. He looked steadily at Jan and then said to the soldier, 'Take him to the ship. I will give his case further thought.'

There was a long silence. Jan couldn't breathe. The soldier pushed him back, muttering, 'Should be made an example of... a mutineer is a mutineer.' Dragging Jan along roughly, he threw him in a boat which rowed him out to the *Sardam*.

As Jan climbed on board, he saw the preacher's daughter Judith on deck, talking to Lucretia. They looked at him, amazed.

'Reprieved at the last moment,' said the soldier. 'The Commander went all soft on him.'

Judith looked at Jan. 'You were kind once to my baby brother, Jan Pelgrom,' she said. 'May God have mercy on you.'

Jan was taken below and shackled. He huddled in a corner, shaking.

For days Jan was kept there, not knowing his fate. A soldier brought him food and water and emptied his piss bucket, but he was a surly man and Jan could get little information from him.

Above, the ship was a hive of activity. Now that the trials and hangings were over, the Commander was sending men to salvage everything they could from the islands, especially precious cargo from *Batavia*. Every item was listed meticulously and stored on board. Pelsaert was a loyal Company man and it was his duty to save what he could for the Company.

Jan wondered if he had been forgotten. He saw no one apart from the soldier who fed him.

Then one day, all the surviving mutineers came back from Seals' Island. Among them was Wouter.

'What's going to happen to you, Wouter?' asked Jan. 'Has the Commander told you?'

Wouter shook his head. 'No, nothing,' he said gruffly.

'Why have they brought you on board?'

Wouter shrugged. 'They say we are to set sail for Java soon.'

The days passed, and preparations were being made for the *Sardam*'s voyage.

One morning, Wouter and Jan were called to the Commander's cabin. Pelsaert looked up from his writing table as they were brought in.

'You know that we are about to make sail back to Java?' he said.

'Aye, sir,' said Jan and Wouter in unison.

Pelsaert fiddled with the seal on his desk. 'I have decided your fate, Wouter Looes,' he said at last.

Wouter stood to attention, only a slight twitch beneath one eye betraying any emotion.

'Sir?'

'I have thought long about this, Wouter. Your crimes are as bad as those of the other mutineers, but there was one passenger who pleaded for your life to be spared. So,' said Pelsaert, putting his long fingers together as if in prayer, 'you are to live.'

Jan glanced at Wouter, and saw his shoulders drop with relief.

'However,' continued Pelsaert, 'You will not come back with us to Java.'

Wouter looked puzzled. 'Am I to stay here, sir?' he asked.

'No. I have decided that you shall be marooned on the South Land, Wouter Looes. Though you are a murderer and a mutineer, you are a leader of men, that much is clear. You are resourceful and you will find a way to survive and make contact with the Aborigines there.'

Wouter said nothing for a moment. Then

he cleared his throat. 'And if.I find my way back to Java?'

'You will not find your way back to Java,' said the Commander, firmly. 'Your orders are to stay on the South Land. Other ships will pass this way and, who knows, you may be able to make contact with them. If so, then the Company would be interested to learn more of this unknown land and its people.'

'Yes, sir,' said Wouter.

The Commander grunted. 'We shall cast you off in an inlet we have already visited. You will have a yawl and plenty of provisions.'

Wouter nodded. Then Pelsaert turned to Jan.

'And you, Jan Pelgrom de Bye,' he said.

Jan held his breath.

'You shall be his companion.'

Wouter looked up sharply, and Jan saw the dismay in his eyes.

Jan couldn't speak. His head was a muddle of emotions. He was not to die – at least, not yet – but how would they survive, the two of them, in the great empty, unknown South Land? Just a few provisions, in a hostile country with wild natives, and probably a slow and painful death at the end of it all.

'Dismissed,' said Pelsaert.

But it was some days before Jan and Wouter were cast adrift. The captain of the *Sardam* and four companions had gone missing. Pelsaert had sent them to look for any valuable flotsam left on the islands and they had not returned. Up and down the *Sardam* went, searching the waters, but there was no sign of them. A fierce wind had got up on the day they set out, and it was feared that their boat had turned over.

Wouter and Jan sat side by side, in leg irons, surrounded by the mutineers who were going back to Java to be tried there. No one spoke much.

'Maybe the Captain and his companions reached the shore,' said Jan.

Wouter sighed. 'Maybe.'

Day after day, Pelsaert searched for them, but at last he gave up and in mid-November, on a beautiful calm day, the *Sardam* sailed into an inlet close to the shore and dropped anchor.

Jan and Wouter were brought up on deck and their leg irons removed. They looked at each other – both pale young men, yet so different from each other. Wouter was a strong and well-built soldier of twenty-four; Jan, a puny youth of eighteen.

The yawl had been provisioned and lay alongside. Pelsaert and a few others were on deck to see them go.

Pelsaert nodded towards the shore. 'Look,' he said. 'From here you can clearly see a river.'

Jan shaded his eyes, but he could see nothing.

'There,' said Wouter, pointing. 'I see it, sir. There it is.'

Jan followed the direction of Wouter's finger and at last he saw a clearly defined channel which passed around a steep point before flowing into the dune land and making its way to the sea.

'We'll make camp near the river, sir,' said Wouter.

Pelsaert nodded, and beckoned the preacher forward.

Reluctantly, the preacher came towards them, scarcely able to conceal his distaste, and Jan remembered that terrible evening when he had forced the man to drink goblet after goblet of wine while Wouter and the others were murdering his family. He bent his head. He couldn't meet the preacher's eyes.

'May God go with you and preserve your souls.'

Jan and Wouter climbed down into the yawl and as soon as they were cast off, he heard Pelsaert shout to one of the sailors, 'Weigh anchor and set course for Java.'

As he and Wouter fought to keep the loaded boat afloat, Jan took one last last look at the *Sardam*. The anchor was pulled up, the sails hoisted and the ship started to move away.

A solitary figure stood at the rail. Lucretia was looking after them, her hand raised in silent farewell.

PART TWO
MAROONED

Chapter Eight

Jan

A soldier and a cabin boy. Neither of us knows how to handle a boat, and we shout and swear at each other as the craft spins and plunges. We have been given a barrel of biscuits and other victuals, some tools for making camp, three blankets, a musket and shot, a few trinkets to trade and a supply of water and wine, and all this rolls and pitches in the bottom of the boat as she is flung through the waves. It is not far to the shore, so we don't put up the sail. Wouter is far stronger than me and he takes the paddle.

'Watch out for any rocks or reefs, Jan, and steer the boat. That will be your job,' he shouts, trying to make himself heard above the sound of the waves.

I try to look out for hazards ahead, but it is hard to steer with the pole *and* stay in the boat, so I almost miss spotting some.

Then: 'Rocks! Rocks on the starboard side!' I shout.

Just in time, Wouter puts out the paddle to stop the boat crashing into the jagged rocks.

I try to steer the boat, but I am no sailor and it bucks and turns under my hand. The salt spray is over me and I wipe my stinging eyes. We are closer in now, among the great rolling waves crashing on the shore.

Wouter says something, but I don't hear him over the sound of the breaking waves. Suddenly he drops the paddle and lurches towards me, grabbing the steering pole.

'Take the paddle, damn you!' he yells. 'If you can't steer the vessel, then row instead.'

I scramble over him and grab the paddle.

'Now row, Jan! Row with all your strength.'

I grit my teeth. I plunge the paddle into the water and try to steady the craft as it heads for the shore. I feel pain in my hands. I don't have the gnarled, hard hands of a sailor and the rough paddle is stripping my skin, the salt burning my raw flesh.

The surf is breaking around us and we are crashing with it towards the beach.

'Hold on, Jan,' shouts Wouter. 'This surf is wild.'

Then I cry out, 'We've hit a reef!' as I feel the boat jar against something.

Wouter laughs out loud. 'It's not a reef, you stupid boy,' he says. 'It is sand. We've reached the shallow water. God be praised, we've reached the shore of the Southern Land.'

We climb out into the shallows and between us manage to drag the boat on to the sand and beach it.

'We've done it, Jan!' yells Wouter, flinging himself down on the sand.

I raise my bleeding hands to the sky and echo his words.

Then Wouter sees my hands.

'Take your shirt off, boy,' he says gruffly. 'Tear it with your teeth and wrap the cloth round your hands.'

I pull my shirt over my head. Pelsaert ordered us to wash and gave us clean clothes before setting out so, for the first time in months I smell better and am wearing fresh linen. But I don't hesitate. I rip the new shirt into bandages for my hands.

When I am more comfortable, I look about me and the excitement I felt when we landed starts to drain away. This is a desolate place. There are no trees, no birds – just white sand and a few scrubby bushes among the dunes.

'Where is the river?' I ask stupidly.

Wouter gestures to the north. 'Up there, round the point,' he says.

He tells me to search round for driftwood, but it is not easy to find and our fire, when it is lit, doesn't last long enough for us to cook on it.

'Why did you light it?' I say to Wouter as he sits by the fire looking out to sea. 'You could see it was too small to cook on.'

'You'll be glad of the warmth from the embers at night, Jan,' he says, poking at it and watching as the flame flares for a moment. 'And I told the lady I'd light a fire.'

'The lady Lucretia?' I ask.

'Aye. I promised her that I'd light a fire to let her know we are safely landed.'

'She won't see it from this distance.'

He looks sad. 'Probably not.' He knows he will never see her again.

We drink a little water and eat some of the biscuits

from the barrel, and then we settle down to sleep. I wrap myself in one of the blankets, but it is sodden with seawater and I fling it off and move near the warmth of the dying fire.

When I wake, Wouter is still sleeping, stretched out like a starfish beside the dead fire. I get up slowly, my swollen hands still raw, and search for more driftwood for our fire. I am hungry, and plan to cook something for the two of us. If I learned nothing else on that island of death, I did learn to find food and cook it.

I walk a long way before I find more driftwood and drag it back. Then I try to strike the tinder-box with a flint, but my hands are too swollen. I fling the box down and go off to see if I can find some shellfish. But there are no rock-pools nearby, so I come back to the camp empty-handed and in low spirits.

Wouter is awake when I return and has laid out our provisions on the ground and rekindled the fire.

'Look, Jan,' he says cheerfully. 'We shall not starve for a while. There is black bread, salt pork, flour , biscuits, cheese and salt, as well as two sealed jugs of wine.'

Some of the food has been damaged by the sea but my spirits improve as I help Wouter prepare a meal. We have a small iron cooking-pan amongst our provisions and I show him how to make flour cakes with the flour and water.

As we eat, the sun grows stronger and my fair skin reddens. I am no longer hardened against the sun, having been kept below deck on the *Sardam* these past weeks.

Wouter looks at me. 'We need to make some shade here,' he says. 'We can't spend all day in this sun.'

'We could make the sail into a tent – as we did on the island,' I suggest.

We find a stout branch lying on the sand and Wouter drives it into the ground with the blunt side of our small axe. Then we spread the sailcloth over it and huddle underneath, hauling all the foodstuff in with us.

'What else have we got?' I ask.

Wouter counts our goods off on his fingers:

'A spade, an axe, flints and tinderbox, a burning glass, a lantern, two jars of ointment, two shirts and two pairs of breeches, two hats, a roll of thread with needles, the cooking-pan, water and food. Oh, and a journal with a set of quills and some ink.'

'And the trading goods?'

'Pelsaert has listed toys, knives, beads, little bells and small mirrors,' he says, 'but I've not opened the trading chest. We can look later.'

We are quiet after we have eaten. Now that we are on our own, we are awkward with each other. Wouter smears some of the ointment on my hands and tells me to rest.

'When we are rested, I shall explore. We only have a small barrel of water and we must find the river if we are to survive.'

I nod. 'Wouter?'

'Yes.'

I hang my head.

'Well, what is it?' he asks gruffly.

'Shall we ever be forgiven for what we have done?'

Wouter looks at me and frowns. 'Don't mention the past, Jan. Think to the future. Think how we shall survive now. What happened on those islands was madness.'

I swipe a fly away with my sticky hands. 'We all

followed him, Wouter. We all believed Corneliez,' I mutter.

Wouter turns on me angrily. 'Don't mention his name, Jan,' he says, and spits on to the sand. 'Aye, we believed him, fools that we were. We thought he would lead us to a better life.'

'There were so many killed.' I shudder at the memory.

Wouter takes me by the shoulders and shakes me.

'Stop it, Jan. You will drive us both mad. It was a matter of kill or be killed. You know that. And I am a soldier. Killing is what I do.'

'But…' I faltered. I couldn't find the words to tell him how I'd enjoyed the power, enjoyed seeing the fear others had of me, how I'd even got a taste for killing.

His voice interrupts my thoughts. 'For pity's sake, be quiet, Jan! We shall not speak of it again. We have enough troubles. We must make plans.'

I nod silently.

A little later, Wouter sets off to search for the river and I am left at our camp. I have begged him to let me go with him but he wouldn't allow it.

'Use your head, Jan. We only have a little water.

If both of us go, we shall use double rations. No, you must stay here and guard our supplies.'

'But what if I am attacked?'

Wouter shrugs. 'If anyone attacks you, you will have plenty of warning, Jan,' he says, and suddenly he smiles and throws out his arms. 'See, there is nowhere here for an attacker to hide, to come upon you unawares.'

'But…'

'Enough! You cannot come with me. I am stronger than you and the heat does not bother me as it does you. I shall return later when I have found water.'

'What if you don't return?'

Wouter loses patience. 'If I don't return, boy, then I shall have been killed and you must make your own way.'

Sullenly, I creep back into our makeshift tent.

Wouter takes some of the water and sets off along the shoreline to the north. I watch him until his figure is just a dot in the distance. When I can see him no more, I am left alone with nothing but my thoughts to plague me and again I see the face of the cabin boy I killed and the faces of the others, too. But most of all, I remember the smile of the preacher's youngest boy as he stretched out his hands to greet me – and the married woman who gave herself to me to save her daughter.

I know that I shall never be forgiven. On board *Batavia,* the preacher used to read passages from the Bible every day at prayers and there is one phrase which sticks in my mind: *Vengeance is mine, saith the Lord.* Vengeance! The preacher explained what it meant. Will God take vengeance on us for our crimes?

I sleep for a while, but my dreams are full of horrors and I'm glad to wake up again.

I find one of the hats and ram it on my head, then I put on one of the shirts we've been given. Thus protected from the sun, I wander about the beach collecting any driftwood I can find and drag it back to camp. It is hot work but I dare drink only a few sips of water.

I try to open the clasps on the trading chest, but my hands are still swollen and clumsy.

I pick up the journal and look at its blank pages. If only I could write, I would tell what has happened. Maybe Wouter will teach me my letters.

I fling the journal aside and go out again. This time I climb to the top of the nearest dune and shade my eyes to look towards the steep hill we saw from the *Sardam*. I can make out a ridge on the other side of the hill, so the river must flow through the valley between the two.

I stay there a little while hoping to see Wouter coming back, but it is much hotter away from the sea so I return to the boat and the shelter of the sail.

As the day wears on, I become more and more certain that Wouter has been attacked and killed by some wild animal or by hostile Aborigines.

I pace up and down the shoreline staring in the direction Wouter went, willing him to reappear and tell me he has found the river.

Then, at last, I see a dot in the distance. My heart pounds. Is it Wouter?

My eyes strain and I watch fearfully as the dot turns into a man. It *is* Wouter! I run towards him, arms outstretched.

But as I get close I see that he looks spent. I start to question him but he shakes his head and walks towards the boat. He slumps down in the shade of the sail and takes the leather water bottle off his hip belt. I see that it is still half-full.

'Did you find the river?'

He nods, and continues to drink.

I wait for him to tell me more, but he takes his time and I know better than to press him.

At last he says, 'There's a sand bar across the mouth of the river close to the duneland that makes a lagoon, but the water in it is undrinkable, so I went further round the side of the ridge and I found a fresh waterhole.'

I clap my sore hands. 'So we can make camp there, by the waterhole?' I say.

Wouter picks up a handful of sand and lets it trickle on to the ground through his fingers.

'Perhaps for one night, but then I think we should move further away, follow the river up the valley.'

I frown at him, puzzled.

He goes on. 'There are tracks by the waterhole, Jan.'

'Tracks of animals?'

He nods. 'Some are animal tracks.' He pauses. 'And some are human.'

I stare at him. 'Perhaps it is the others – the Captain from the *Sardam* and the four sailors.'

He is looking down at the ground. 'There are too many footprints for just five men.'

'Then... then are these the Aborigines the Commander spoke of?'

He shrugs. 'I suppose so.'

A shiver of fear passes down my spine.

Wouter shifts his position. 'And there are well trodden paths up into the hills,' he says.

He looks at me as I take this in. So this is not such an empty land, after all. There are humans nearby, humans who come to drink at the waterhole and have made a track up into the hills. For a while we say nothing, but I know what Wouter is thinking. Like me, he is thinking that we may not be welcomed by these Aborigines. Who knows what dangers we face? My mind fills with images of wild savages armed with sharpened sticks and stones descending upon us in a furious pack.

'What are we going to do?' I ask him at last.

Wouter stands up, shaking off his uncertainty as he becomes the soldier again.

'We'll spend one more night here and then, at first light, we'll make for the waterhole. We'll be loaded down, so it will be slow going and we'll have to make camp at the waterhole for one night. After that, we'll strike up into the hills, keeping the river in our sights, and see if we can find a place to make camp on the bank.'

'And the boat?' I ask.

Wouter shrugs. 'We'll have to leave it here. We'll drag it well up above the waterline and hide it.'

Suddenly he grasps my shoulder. 'Come, Jan, take heart. We'll have a feast tonight. We'll drink some of the wine, so at least we can forget our cares. For who knows what tomorrow will bring?'

Chapter Nine

The ointment is working on my hands and the next day they are less sore, but I still protect them with the torn linen before we unload the boat.

At dawn, Wouter opens the chest of trading goods and we look through them. I ring the little bells and handle the knives and beads. Then I unwrap some colourful wooden toys, figures of soldiers and sailors which you can make walk through a system of hooks and wires. I should like to play with them myself, for I never had toys as a child.

'Do you think the Aborigines will like these, Wouter? Do you think they'll be friendly?' I ask.

'How should I know?' he says, and his voice has an edge to it. 'Pelsaert has told us to make friends with the native people, but they may kill us before we have a chance to show them anything.'

I rewrap the toys and replace them in the chest.

Then, sweating and swearing, we take down the mast and drag the boat up into the dunes. When we look back, it has merged with the sand and the brown, windswept, spiky grass.

We smother our fire with sand, then spread the sail on the ground and load all our goods in it, pulling the sail ropes tight so that everything is safe within. Wouter makes a rope harness so that he can drag the sail and its contents behind him, but he strains as he walks forwards. It is too heavy. He loosens the harness and squats down on the ground.

'This is too heavy for one man, Jan. You'll have to carry the trading chest and the musket.'

He unties the sail ropes and takes out the chest and the musket. When he hands the chest to me, I stagger under its weight. Then he unstraps his leather shoulder cross-strap and buckles it over my chest, fixing the musket on it.

I dare not complain, but when we set off again I am out of breath at once, and although our pace is slow, my arms are screaming with pain when we stop for a drink. I put the chest down on the sand

and stretch my aching limbs before taking the water bottle from my belt.

'Not too much, Jan,' warns Wouter. 'We have a way to go before we reach the waterhole.'

I stop in mid-gulp. He is right, but I am so thirsty. Before we set off again, I look back at the way we've come. We've not made much progress, but I'm relieved to see that there is no sign of our boat. We may need it again if the Aborigines drive us away. I close my mind to those thoughts and concentrate on the here and now – getting through the next hour, the next few steps.

Slowly, slowly we creep along the edge of the ocean. The sun is already beating down and I'm glad of my hat and shirt.

I think back to November in Holland – a cold, grey month with bare trees and damp mists rising up from the dykes. But here, in this topsy-turvy world, summer is just beginning and the heat is worse than even the hottest summer's day at home.

My mind and my body start to go numb, but I know I have to keep going. Blindly I follow Wouter, stepping in his footprints on the sand, the sweat pouring down my face and trickling down my back. I am glad that my sore hands are still bound with strips of linen, otherwise I might lose my grasp on the trading chest.

At last we round the point and I have my first sight of the river mouth. It is as Wouter described it: a long sand bar trapping its lower waters into a lagoon of brackish water. Higher up, it can be seen snaking up the valley between steep, tree-lined banks on one side and a high ridge on the other.

I start to salivate as we approach the lagoon, and when I reach it I drop the chest and kneel down beside the water.

'Don't drink here,' says Wouter sharply as I scoop up some of the stagnant water into my hands. I take no notice but before I can drink, he strikes my cheek hard and my hands fly to my face.

'You stupid boy,' he hisses. 'If you drink this, you will be sick. Wait, damn you. Wait until we reach the waterhole.'

I feel like sobbing, with all this water before me.

Wouter kicks me in the rump. 'Get up, boy,' he says sharply. 'We might come upon the Aborigines at any moment.'

When he mentions Aborigines, I stand up, my thirst forgotten. Wouter stands close to me.

'Now,' he says. 'Look up there' – and although

there is no one near to hear us, his voice is a whisper. I follow his gaze, and my heart lurches. For, further up the valley, in the distance, a plume of smoke is rising above the trees, drifting straight up into the blue sky.

We look at each other. 'We are not alone,' says Wouter grimly.

'Perhaps it is the lost captain from the *Sardam*,' I say weakly.

'Perhaps,' says Wouter, 'But I doubt it. They would have kept to the coast so that the *Sardam* could find them. No, I'm sure that the good captain and his men were lost at sea in that storm.'

'Then ... then we must be the only white men in this great South Land.'

Wouter nods. 'So it would seem.'

The going becomes harder as we make our way round the bottom of the ridge which plunges down to the water's edge. There are great slabs of slippery rock here, and it is difficult to keep my balance as I carry the chest. When I take my eyes off my feet, I stare into the rock pools and see movement within them. Perhaps there are shellfish we can eat. Wouter is making slow progress with the loaded sail. I have to put down the chest and help him carry the sail over the jagged rocks so that it does not tear open.

Our water supply has nearly gone, and I ask Wouter how far it is to the waterhole.

'Not far now, Jan.'

He takes a final swig from his water bottle, and points. I see a bare patch amidst the vegetation, and now I can make out the paths which wind down to it from the hills above.

'We'll camp there for the night.'

'What if the savages come while we are there?'

Wouter snaps at me. 'We need water, we are exhausted and I cannot drag this damn sail any further today, so we have little choice.'

I keep quiet, and soon we are on our way again, shuffling with our awkward loads towards the waterhole. It is much further away than it looks and when we finally reach it, we are both parched.

Wouter is right, there are footprints all round the hole, many of the impressions baked hard, but some are fresh, sunk into the mud and not yet dried by the sun. I look round in every direction but there is no sound, no sight of another human being. Yet I feel as if I am being watched.

Wouter flings himself down on his stomach and

starts to scoop water into his mouth. I have a better idea. I take the iron pan from inside the sail, dip it in the water and hand it to him. Wouter looks up at me and smiles, his first smile all day.

'Well, Jan,' he says. 'You have *some* good sense, then.'

We find some flat ground a little way from the waterhole, shaded by trees, and make camp. The trees here are tall and straight and their bark hangs off them in untidy strips. When we are settled, I lie back and look up through the branches, listening to the dry rustle of the undergrowth. But my peace is soon disturbed as I am suddenly bitten by some vicious insect. I leap up and see an ants' nest beneath me.

'Look at the size of them, Wouter!' I gasp, rubbing my leg. 'They are giants!'

Wouter laughs. 'What a child you are, Jan, to be bothered by a few ants.'

But he wasn't the one who was bitten.

He goes on. 'This is a good place. We have water and shade and no doubt animals will come here to drink. We may yet have fresh meat.'

My mouth waters at the thought of meat. On the island we only had seals and seabirds to eat. In time, we may be able to kill some of those furry, jumping beasts that Wiebbe and his soldiers ate, but for now I take the salt pork, black bread and cheese from the sail and we swill this down with wine from the flagon we broached yesterday.

There are plenty of dry branches scattered beneath the trees and the flints and tinderbox are still dry, so we soon have a merry fire going. As the sun begins to sink, there is a noise in the trees above us and chattering, brightly coloured parrots come in to roost. I stare up at them, wondering whether they would be good to eat.

Warmed by the food and wine, and knowing that we have water to drink, I want to talk, but I get little response from Wouter. He tells me to save my strength and sleep.

I lie staring up at the sky and wonder at the stars – so different from the night sky in Holland. Is Lucretia looking up at this sky on board the *Sardam*? Does she think of us – of Wouter – and wonder whether we will live or die?

We have done everything together today. We cannot part company now that we are in this strange new land. Like most soldiers and sailors on *Batavia*, Wouter despises me, but he is stuck with me, however much he dislikes the fact – and I, for my part, would rather be with him than with many of the other mutineers.

I sleep at last, too tired to worry about what the next day will bring.

I wake as the sun is rising and lie still listening to the birdsong, but I am conscious of something else – some other presence. Slowly I raise myself on one elbow and look towards the waterhole.

And then I see them: the strange animals that the soldiers on High Island talked of – the animals whose meat kept Weibbe Hayes and his soldiers alive. I found it hard to believe the men's stories, but now I see the creatures with my own eyes.

Several of them are drinking from the waterhole, but as soon as I move, they hear me and bound away, startled. I have never seen any animal like these, with their huge, strong back legs, their long faces with large eyes, their furry ears and tiny, shrunken forepaws.

When he wakes, I tell Wouter about the animals, and he laughs.

'Now we shall have water *and* meat, Jan.'

We coax our fire into life again and make more flour cakes, before repacking our belongings into the sail. Then we fill our water bottles and set off, following one of the steep tracks that leads from the waterhole up into the wooded hills.

Our progress is even slower now. Wouter cannot drag the sail along the narrow path, so we have put the musket and the trading chest back inside the sail and are carrying the ungainly load between us, shuffling forward at a snail's pace. And all the time, the sounds of the birds surround us. Such strange sounds! One bird cry is like a faint, persistent bell, another is a raucous laugh, and always there are flashes of colour – red, blue and green – as the parrots dart between the trees. And in the background the constant sound of the river below us.

All day we plod forward. Each time I spot a good place to make camp, Wouter finds fault with it. The ground is too uneven, it is too close to the river bank, too far away from it, too crowded in with trees, too exposed. I try to reason with him, but he snaps at me.

'It must be perfect, Jan,' he says, wiping the sweat

from his brow. 'We are looking for somewhere to make our home.'

Home! Are we to call this strange land our home?

Then, at last, we come round a bend and before us is a huge sandy hollow, shaded by trees but not too dark. Wouter stops, and I hold my breath.

'Here?'

He nods. 'See Jan, it was worth the wait.' He stands on the edge of the hollow, and points to the flat centre. 'We shall build a hut here, and make a garden where we can grow vegetables.'

Vegetables! He is mad. We are not in gentle Dutch farming country now. But I keep quiet and help him heave our goods into the centre of the hollow.

He is right, though. This is an ideal spot, and it is pleasing to hear the sound of the rushing water in the river below.

Wouter unties the sail and takes out all our goods, piling them up neatly, then we tie the sail between trees to give us shelter. When we have done this, Wouter tells me to start making a fire, but as I scrape away the sandy soil to make a place for it, I see that the sand is discoloured by old ash.

Today I have been in good spirits, but now the fear returns.

'Wouter,' I say, and point at the ground. 'There is old ash here.'

He squats down and picks the ash up. 'Then we are not the first to use this place, Jan.'

I nod, and a shiver goes through my body. I hope that whoever used this place before us will not come back to claim it.

Chapter Ten

I know that they are around us, the Aborigines. Days have passed and we have not seen them yet, but they leave us signs.

One morning, I notice unfamiliar footprints close to our fire. They must have come silently, for they did not disturb our sleep. Did they watch while we slept? If so, what did they make of these two fair-skinned Dutchmen? Next time, will they come with spears and kill us?

Another morning, we wake to find a beautiful conch shell laid on the ground on top of a long piece of bark. I pick it up and stroke its smooth surface. I am sure that to the Aborigines this is treasure. What does it mean? Are they welcoming us with a precious gift? I show it to Wouter, and he frowns.

'Why don't they show themselves?' he says. 'It makes me uneasy that they come when we are sleeping. I would rather see them face to face.'

For the next few days, we try every way we can think of to trap the jumping furry animals, but they are too quick for us. At first it seems like a game, but as our food supplies dwindle it becomes more serious. We need meat to survive.

'I shall have to use the musket, Jan,' says Wouter at last.

We only have a small supply of shot and Wouter wants to preserve it, but we need to eat. Wouter is worried, too, about what the Aborigines will make of the loud report of a gun. Will it anger them? Will it drive them away?

That night, as we sit round our fire eating salt pork, Wouter makes a decision.

'I shall go back to the waterhole and camp there tonight,' he says. 'Then, when the creatures come to drink at dawn, I shall have a clear shot at them. It will be easier there. Here, there's too much vegetation where they can hide.'

'I'll come too, then,' I say quickly, but he shakes his head.

'One of us must stay here and guard our things,' he says firmly.

After we have eaten, Wouter shoulders the gun. and, wrapping one of the blankets round his shoulders, he sets off holding the lantern before him, following the path back to the waterhole.

I am left alone with only the light of the fire. Everywhere I sense movement in the darkness. I know that there is no one there, but my mind makes the splashing of the river into the sound of whispering voices and the light breeze in the treetops into the rattle of clashing spears. I get up and walk to the edge of the hollow, away from the trees, and look up at the sky. The sailors on *Batavia* could sail by these stars, but the night sky here is a mystery to me. I only know our position because we are near the mouth of a river which spills out on to the Western coast of the great South Land. If we went further inland I should get lost, for the stars would be no help to me.

I walk back to the fire, bank up the embers and lie down on the sand nearby, wrapped in my blanket.

I wake early, when the pale light of dawn is just touching the trees and rocks and the sun has no warmth in it. It feels strange without Wouter, and I wonder whether he will be able to shoot us some meat. I walk into the trees to collect more firewood, to where the steep bank plunges down to the river, and I stand there for a while, watching as the light begins to strengthen and sparkle on the water.

A slight movement upstream catches my eye. I stand stock-still, clutching my bundle of firewood, my heart hammering in my chest – and stare. Coming round the bend of the river, moving rapidly downstream, is a boat! A rough canoe. Is it made of bark or a hollowed-out tree? I cannot tell. It is being steered by a man who doesn't need to row because the river is fast, but he plunges his paddle expertly into the water, first on this side, then the other, keeping a straight course. I watch him as he passes beneath me, but he is too far away to see clearly. I can see only that he is black and naked.

Suddenly, there is the unmistakable sound of the musket being fired. I jump at the noise, even though I know what it is. But the man in the canoe does not. At the sound of the gun, his head spins this way and that, and then it jerks up to the sky. He drops his paddle, leaps out of the canoe and makes for the bank, dragging the craft behind him. I watch as he scrambles out on the far side, abandons the canoe at the river's edge and bounds into the undergrowth out of sight.

Even from this distance I sense his terror. He has never heard a gunshot before.

I revive the fire so that the smoke rises and billows, keeping the mosquitoes at bay, then I stack the rest of the firewood and settle down to wait. But I am restless and long to tell Wouter about the man in the canoe, so I walk a little way down the track. There is no sign of him so I retrace my steps, for I know he will be angry if I don't stay near the camp.

Yesterday we started to cut and shape branches to make a frame for our hut. I sit down cross-legged and go on with the work, choosing long, flexible sticks and sharpening the ends so that they will sink easily into the soft ground. We have plenty of fallen branches but many are dry and break too easily. As I look up at the trees which surround the camp, I am struck again by the great strips of bark which hang from them. Perhaps we can use this bark to build our hut. I pull at a long piece and it comes away easily enough. Idly, I start to weave it in and out of some of the sticks I have prepared. I sit back on my haunches observing my work, dreaming of a solid, well-built hut.

And it is as I am sitting there, alone with my thoughts, that I see him. It takes a while for my eyes to adjust to the darkness among the trees away to my right, but slowly I am aware of being watched. I have often had this feeling – we both have – but we have never seen the watcher. This time I see him clearly, and I sense that he wants me to see him, for he is standing very still and holds a long spear in one hand.

Although my heart is banging against my ribcage, I stay motionless and take a good look at him. He is small and naked with black skin and black, curly hair which almost covers his eyes, and I notice his wide nostrils and high cheekbones. He looks different from the natives we saw in Africa.

We stare at each other. I dare not move, although I am starting to get cramp in my legs. I wish I knew what to do. Should I raise my hand in greeting, or would he see that as an unfriendly gesture?

Slowly, I get to my feet, my eyes never leaving his face. Still he doesn't move. Now I am standing alone and unprotected, and I see his eyes slide to my clothes. What can he be making of my cabin-boy shirt and trousers?

I take a step towards him – and still he does not move – but then I hear twigs snapping in the distance and the faint sound of Wouter's tuneless whistling. For an instant I turn my head in the direction of the waterhole, and when I turn back the black man has gone, melted into the trees.

The sound of whistling comes closer and Wouter emerges. He is carrying a small furry beast over one shoulder and his musket is slung round the other. He crashes into the centre of the camp and drops the beast to the ground. He is in high good humour.

'There, Jan. This fellow will keep us in food for a while.'

He tells me how he lay in wait until the animals came to the waterhole.

'Just as well my shot was true, Jan,' he says. 'Once they heard my musket, the animals vanished.'

I tell him about the man in the canoe and the man in the trees, and he looks thoughtful.

'We must conserve our shot, Jan. We don't want to terrify these Aborigines. We must learn to fish, and to find roots and berries.'

But for the moment we have meat to eat, and I spend the morning skinning and chopping up the creature and salting some of the meat to preserve it.

Then I build up the fire and make a rough spit from forked branches, suspending the rest of the carcass over the heat, speared through with a stout stick.

That evening we eat greedily, our bellies satisfied for the first time in months. We have a little more wine to celebrate our kill and Wouter praises me both for my cooking skills and for my idea of weaving bark between the stakes of our hut.

The next day, both full of energy, we make good progress and the hut begins to take shape, although it looks too flimsy to protect us when winter comes. I wonder about this, and start to think back to the daub used in the walls of my family's home in Bemmel. Taking the iron pan, I make my way down the steep bank to the river's edge and scoop up a load of sludge, then climb back up to our camp.

Wouter frowns at me. 'What are you doing, boy?'

I don't answer. It is easier to show him. I smear the mud thickly over an area of sticks and bark, making a smooth outside surface.

'See,' I say. 'It will hold the bark and the branches in place and make it warmer. And we can cover the mud with clods of earth for roofing.'

Wouter nods. And without a word he strips a long piece of bark off a nearby tree and heads for the river. So, with the cooking pan and the bark, we toil to and from the river with our cargo of sludge. After the first trip we discard our clothes, which are becoming mud-stained, and by the end of the day we are so covered in mud that we are almost black, so we sluice ourselves clean in the river.

Our hut is coming on well, we have food to eat – for the moment, at least – and we are cleaner than we ever were on board *Batavia.*

As the sun sets on this strange country, its dying rays turn the rocks from grey to orange.

'It is as if the land is on fire.' I don't know if I say this out loud or if it is only in my head, but Wouter doesn't answer me. He has taken out the journal that Pelsaert has given us and is turning its pages.

'Will you write in it, Wouter?' I ask.

He shrugs, and tosses it away. 'I am no writer, Jan. And who would read it, anyway?'

Soon, weary from all the work, I doze, and my mind wanders. At first, back to my life in Holland with my mother, aged before her time by poverty and child-bearing. Will she care, if she hears what has happened to me? Will anyone? Then to my time on *Batavia.* The Under Merchant is with me now – too close – sometimes friendly, sometimes mad, with staring eyes, striding about the deck in his red and gold cloak, then screaming and choking on the gibbet.

I shiver, and reach for my blanket. I was in thrall to that man! But I was not alone. All those who did his bidding killed for him without a second thought, believing his promise of a better life and riches in the Indies. Were they all, like me, half-crazed and filled with blood lust? We all obeyed him without hesitating. Even Wouter! On the one hand he was protecting Lucretia from harm, and on the other, carrying out the Under Merchant's orders to slaughter the innocent family of the preacher. And yet, throughout these past days Wouter has cared for me – an ignorant, stupid, good-for-nothing cabin boy. Without his protection I would have perished.

Wouter tells me not to think about what happened on those islands. But I can't forget. However busy I keep myself, thoughts crowd in on me and my dreams are terrifying.

Chapter Eleven

Wouter

I try to keep track of time, but the days merge into each other and I find it hard. We must have been here for two months at least, and it is now high summer. We were right to camp here in the shade of the trees and close to the river.

The camp is well established now. We have a good-sized hut and it protects us and our goods, but God, how I long for company! When Pelsaert first told me I was to be lumbered with the half-crazed cabin boy, I would rather have been hanged out there on the island with the rest of them.

I forbid Jan to speak of those dreadful days, but I can't help thinking about them myself.

Things could have turned out so differently. If Weibbe Hayes had not reached the *Sardam* first and told Pelsaert that we were coming, we would have taken the ship by surprise, overpowered the crew and sailed away. We were winning the battle on High Island – it was only a matter of time before they were beaten. But then, what would our lives have been like, sailing the seas as pirates with Corneliez? Now that we are away from him I recognise his madness – and the madness of his scheme.

And what will my life be like now, burdened with this boy? On the island he was a menace, screaming threats, puffed up with importance because he was under the protection of Corneliez. Corneliez would have tired of him in the end, no doubt, but it amused him to see the boy flaunt his newfound authority and terrorize the poor passengers – some revenge, I suppose, for having been treated as scum all his life.

I have to admit, Jan has calmed down now and made himself useful. He is, after all, a country boy from Bemmel and he understands the land better than I. I would not have thought of plastering the roof of our hut with mud from the river, nor of weaving the bark between the poles, and I would not have recognised that the ground vines growing near our camp have edible roots deep below the surface. Those roots have been a godsend. Jan digs them out with our spade, slices off the greenery and roasts them in the hot ashes of the fire. When they are split open, the flesh is sweet and flavoursome and they go well with the meat of the strange furry creatures.

A few days ago, I sent Jan back to the sea to scour the rock pools for shellfish. He set off early with a large dish made of bark, and as the afternoon wore on I worried about him and started to walk down towards the sea. But he was unharmed, and I met him returning with his rough bowl full to the brim with live shellfish which he then proceeded to cook, as he had learned to do for Corneliez.

Our diet is better now than it was on board ship and certainly better than when we were prisoners on the island and on the *Sardam*. My scabs and sores are healing. I feel stronger, with more energy.

The change in Jan is startling. His face is clear of spots and he is growing before my eyes. He is changing from a boy into a man. His muscles are thickening with all the physical work we are doing and his pallor has gone. We hardly bother with clothes now, and our bodies are bronzed from the sun. Most evenings, we climb down to the river's edge, fill our water bottles and the trusty iron pan with water for the camp, then wash our bodies. We are cleaner than we have been for months and I am growing a mighty beard! Jan's long hair is bleached blond by the sun and his chin has started to sprout some hair, much to his delight!

At first, we were driven mad by the mosquitoes and flies around us but we have grown accustomed to these and keep up a constant swatting motion with our hands.

Although Jan insists that he saw two Aboriginal men when I was away at the waterhole the first time I shot one of the furry beasts, I have seen nothing of them, although we know they are all around us. They have not visited our camp at night since those early days, but we see smoke rising from their fire a little way up-river and often we sense that they are somewhere nearby, watching us. Are they waiting for us to approach them? Jan is sure that they will be friendly. I am not so confident. But we must make a move soon, for I suspect we may need their help when winter comes and the musket shot runs out.

So far, we have failed to catch a single fish. There is nothing in our supplies to use as a net and even Jan is stumped.

Every day, now, the boy pesters me to seek out the Aborigines. 'We should go and find their camp, Wouter,' he says, but I always make some excuse: 'We must not leave our own camp unprotected,' or, 'We need to salt more meat today.'

I have even started to write in the journal Pelsaert gave us, pretending that I am recording our daily progress – anything to put off visiting the Aboriginal camp. Fortunately, Jan is unlettered and cannot understand that what I write is only a rough description of how we have made our hut and found food and water. But I have little learning and I find making the letters laborious.

Jan watches me write and wants me to teach him his letters, but I am no teacher and I suspect he would be a poor student.

'What are you writing there, Wouter?' he asks. 'What are you saying about me?'

I grunt some reply.

I know that we must contact the Aborigines soon, but I am afraid. I am afraid of their strangeness, afraid that we shall not be able to make ourselves understood, afraid that they will slaughter us. It is curious that I, a soldier whose life has been filled with death and violence, should be less eager to embrace the unknown than an unlettered, foolish cabin boy.

But we must make a move soon.

Chapter Twelve

Jan

We have made a good camp here and we are eating well. I am getting stronger by the day and beginning to grow at last. It is a good feeling running my hand over the downy growth of beard on my chin.

I long to explore and make contact with the Aborigines, but Wouter says we should wait for them to come to us, and that one of us must always be here to guard the camp. I would like to go on my own, but Wouter says I need his protection – and that of his musket.

Our supply of flour has nearly run out and I wonder if grain grows anywhere in this place from which we can make more. It would be good to have a change from meat and roots. Time and again I attempt to fish the river. I try spearing fish with a sharpened stick but the river is fast flowing and I never succeed. I need some sort of net with which to trap them.

One day, at the river's edge, tired from my unsuccessful attempts at fishing, I lie back on a rock with my feet dangling in the water and doze off.

At one point I wake and open my eyes – then close them again quickly, hoping I am still dreaming. But it is no dream. There, on the rock only a few feet away from me, basking in a patch of sunlight which filters through the branches, lies a dragon!

I freeze in horror. It *must* be a dragon. What else could it be, with its scaly skin and long blue tongue which flickers in and out of its mouth? I start to scrabble away from it but as soon I move, the dragon slithers away into the undergrowth.

It is the first time I have seen such a creature in this land of strange birds and animals, and my thudding heart takes a while to return to its normal pace. And when it does, and I can observe my surroundings without panic, I notice something else. On another rock a little way distant lies a strange-looking net! Is it for me? Cautiously, I make my way over to it, pick it up and turn it over in my hands.

I cannot help smiling. It is so simple. Why did I not think to make one like this? It is made from the tough vines that grow on the ground and swarm up the trees. Stripped of their leaves, the vines are strong and pliant and these have been woven together. The net is long and not very deep, so I realise that it stretches across the river to trap fish as they swim downstream. The net was not there before I settled down to sleep, so perhaps someone has been watching me try to fish – and left me a present!

I look round and, as usual, there is no one to be seen, but I take heart from what I hope is a gesture of friendship and walk upstream, hoping to find another of these nets in use so that I can examine it to see how it is attached.

I hug the net to my chest, thinking of the fish we will eat and wondering who has left it for me to find. I keep a careful watch on the ground; we have been here long enough to know that snakes live by the river and we don't know if they are harmful or not. Overhead, the parrots shriek and every now and then I shade my eyes and squint up to watch them, red and green as they flash through the air and alight on the pale wood of the tall trees.

Several times I stop and peer into the water, but I cannot see another net. When I reach a bend in the river, I sit down on another rock. I have never been further than this and I wonder whether I should turn back. But I would like to find the person who gave me the net. If Wouter were with me, he would stop me, but he is back at the camp. I have already waited too long for him to agree to visit the Aborigines, and now I have a reason to seek them out. I want to thank them and I want to learn how to set the net.

As I walk, I tell myself that the Aborigines won't be there. They won't let me see them and will melt into the trees when they hear me approach, just as they have done before.

I keep walking. The afternoon is well advanced now and Wouter may come down to the river to look for me, but I don't care. Let him come! Let him worry! I walk on, taking no trouble to go quietly, and as I walk, I wonder, as I have wondered so many times before, what these black people make of me – of us, of our fair skin. Will they know that we have come in a ship from another country, or will they think we have dropped from the sky?

It will be many years before I fully understand the shock they felt when they first saw us and their belief, not that we had come from another country, but that we were spirits of their dead ancestors come back to them. The Aborigines, after all, knew no land other than their own, they knew nothing of vast ships carrying men from foreign shores, of goods made of metal, of coins and woven cloth, of jewels, or of the great East India Company!

Even though I understood nothing of this on that momentous day when I walked upriver towards their camp, I was not fearful. My previous glimpses of the two men had not alarmed me and I felt sure that they would not harm me; having their gift of a net made me brave.

'Pig-headed fool,' Wouter would have said. And he did say this later, but that day I felt that the time was right. They had seen us; they knew we had made a camp; they had given us a conch shell; and now they had left a net for us. What I did not know then was that we had made our camp on the very spot on which they held their special tribal gatherings, their *corroborees* when all the local tribes come together to trade and to dance out stories of the spirits, their bodies painted up. Our choice of this spot made them believe even more strongly that we were, indeed, spirits of their ancestors come back to earth.

I walk on, sometimes whistling. Every now and then I stop and listen, but still I hear nothing. However, the smell of smoke is stronger in my nostrils now and I know their camp can't be far away. I walk more slowly, more carefully, aware that any moment I may come upon them. I do not want to frighten them.

The first one I see is a young man, standing in the river bending over a net. He must have heard me approach, but he doesn't look up and I stay where I am, watching him as he takes trapped fish from the net, bangs their heads on a rock and lays them in a piece of bark. Even though my heart is pounding in my chest, I notice how the net is strung across the river and anchored with heavy rocks.

He doesn't look up until the last fish is in the bark platter. Then he picks up the platter, straightens up and stares at me, and despite his brave stance I can see that he is breathing fast and that the hands holding the platter are not quite steady.

I know I must be careful. I am still clutching the net and slowly, I hold it up and show my pleasure by smiling at him. He doesn't smile back, but he starts to walk out of the river holding his fish above his head, his eyes sliding back to me from time to time. He is walking away from me now, and when he reaches the river bank he puts the platter carefully on dry land, before heaving himself out of the water with the help of a stout root at the water's edge. Then he picks up his fish again, climbs up the bank and disappears into the trees.

I sit down to wait. What will he say to the others? Will more of them come down from the camp to look at me?

Time passes, and the sun is going down. No one has come to stare at me, but I don't want to turn back now. In any case, soon it will be too dark to find my way downriver.

I am stiff with sitting still and waiting. At last I make up my mind. Before I lose courage, I set off up the steep bank into the trees, following the path taken by the young man. I can smell the smoke from their camp fire so I know I must be close to them. I stride forward with no attempt at stealth, snapping twigs underfoot so that they will hear me approach and not be surprised by me. And although I don't feel very merry, I start whistling again, hoping that this will show them that I mean them no harm.

The trees start to thin out and the soil becomes sandy, like the soil around our own camp. I slow down and walk forward more slowly, looking carefully from side to side, wondering if they are hiding in the trees. And then, as I scramble up on to the flat ground, I see it. The Aborigines' camp!

My first reaction is one of pride. Compared to ours, their camp is a mean sort of place. To be sure, there are a few rough huts, but they are not sturdy like ours and they look as though they are not built to last. In the middle of the camp there is a fire with stones around it. I see that the fish are cooking on it and that there are roots like the ones we have gathered roasting in the hot ashes.

I take all this in at a glance, then look at the people in front of me. They have heard me approach and they are all standing to face me. I swallow, and try not to show any fear. I still have the precious net and, again, I hold it before me and smile at them.

I am wearing my sailor's trousers. Often Wouter and I go naked, but I wear the trousers to protect me when I walk through the undergrowth. And although I am overdressed compared to the

Aborigines, I am glad of the trousers now, suddenly shy of my fair body which, even though it is bronzed from the sun, is so different from theirs.

They are smaller than me, even the men, and there are about a dozen of them. I think they are a family group, but I find it difficult to see any likeness between them. I notice that one of the men is a lot older than the others with wrinkled skin, a long beard flecked with white and thin legs; and there is an old woman, too, who I take to be his wife. The others are younger and sturdy. There is a woman nursing a child, a group of children, several young men including the young man from the river, and a young girl whom I suppose to be about fifteen. She is the only one who smiles at me, and I find myself blushing as I take in her nakedness. Her breasts, which are small and firm, are bare and her only covering is a strip of skin which hangs from her waist.

I keep smiling and holding the net out. Out of the corner of my eye I see several long, wooden spears propped up by a tree at the edge of the camp, made from straight branches of wood and sharp pieces of shale bound on to the end with strips of animal skin. There is also a hollowed-out root or branch beside the spears and some curved wooden objects.

I clear my throat and speak to them in my native Dutch, although I know they will not understand me. What do I say? I can't remember, except that I try to explain where I am from. As soon as I have spoken, there is an instant excited chattering. They all talk at once and point at me. Suddenly my legs feel weak, and very slowly I lower myself to the ground and sit cross-legged, looking at them.

This seems to be a signal for action, and the old woman drags a fish from the fire and presents it to me on a piece of bark. Carefully, I place my net on the ground and take the bark platter. I blow on the fish until it cools and then I eat it with my fingers. What a treat to have different meat to eat!

I smile when I have finished, rub my stomach and thank the old woman. Suddenly she starts to laugh, her old body shaking, her hand in front of her mouth, and gradually the others join in, laughing and pointing at me.

Then I have an idea. Going over to a bare patch of sand, I find a stick and scratch a few marks with it. At once the laughing stops and all the Aborigines crowd forward to look.

I am no artist, but I manage to draw the rough

outline of a ship with tall masts and many sails. I point to myself and I point to the image of the ship in the sand. Although they continue to laugh and make gestures, there is no sign that they understand.

Then one of the younger men comes forward. He is holding a broad leaf in his hand and on it are some loathsome-looking grubs. He hands the leaf to me and reluctantly I take it. I feel only disgust for the pale, wriggling creatures and have to force myself not to snatch my hand away. I have no idea what I should do with them.

Then the young man opens his mouth and with his hand makes an obvious gesture that they should be eaten.

Trying not to show horror, I put the grubs into my mouth and tip them down my throat, feeling the wretched things wriggle inside me and holding my hand over my mouth to stop myself from gagging.

It is the right thing to do! I have delighted them, though I cannot understand why. They smile at me, and one of the young men touches me on the shoulder. The old woman shuffles forward and feels the hair on my head, holding up one fair strand and then another, exclaiming and laughing.

Suddenly she reaches for my trousers and, with a shriek, pulls them down to my ankles. I am mortified as all the Aborigines stare, as one, at my manhood, and I wonder what they will do next. But, once satisfied that I am, indeed, a human – and a male – they turn away and chatter among themselves, leaving me to pull up my breeches, a deep blush covering my face.

I catch the eye of the young girl. She is the only one who is still looking at me, and she is giggling behind her hand. I smile at her.

If she knew what I had done on that island of death, she would never return my smile, but she does, and I see her gleaming white teeth as her lips part and notice how her eyes sparkle.

The island! My thoughts fly back to Wouter. It is nearly dark now and I cannot go back to our camp without a lantern. What shall I do?

The Aborigines seem to accept that I will sleep with them. One by one, the women and the old man leave the fire and go into the rough huts, but the young girl lingers and moves a little closer to me. I try to speak to her. I point to my chest.

'Me Jan,' I say.

She chatters away, so I try again, repeating my name until, at last, she makes an attempt to say it herself. 'Meeaan' is the best she can do. I nod in the darkness and she claps her hands together, then jumps up and runs into the hut.

The young men lie down on the sand near the fire and I join them, stretching out under the stars.

Wouter will be very angry when I do not return.

Chapter Thirteen

Wouter

I cannot find the boy. I have been down to the river, but there is no sign of him. Stupid fool! Has he gone looking for the Aborigines without me?

At last I settle down for the night. I don't go into the hut but lie down beside the fire, though I cannot sleep. The boy maddens me, but I have come to rely on his cooking skills and his inbred country instincts.

Damn him to hell! Where is he? Have the savages killed him? Will they come for me now? How many are there? These thoughts crowd into my brain as I lie tossing and turning, one hand always on the musket by my side.

I must have slept at last, for the screeching of the parrots wakes me. There is still no sign of Jan, and I stumble around building up the fire and trying to make cakes in the iron pan with the last of the flour, but I am too impatient to eat and I don't cook them for long enough. They are soggy and unpleasant and they sit heavily in my stomach.

Where *is* the boy? What has happened to him?

Jan

I wake at sunrise and lie still for a few moments listening to the noises around me. The Aborigines are stirring, building up their fire and chattering among themselves. When I sit up and stretch, they all stop talking and look at me.

In years to come, when I understand their language, I know that they were astonished that I was still with them – that I had not vanished back into the spirit world from whence they think I came.

Now that it is light, I can examine the camp and the people, and I begin to see the differences between the family members. They all defer to the old man who, I suppose, is the chief of the tribe, for he is brought food by the others. I notice a collection of berries on a piece of bark – berries that I'd seen before but had not dared to eat in case they were poisonous – and that they are eating these and roasting a dragon on the fire, expertly skinned, just like the one which had so frightened me. They offer me a piece of dragon and its taste is light and good – not as heavy as the meat of the furry creatures.

I know that I must return to Wouter and after I have eaten, I stand up and gesture that I must go. I think that the Aborigines understand my gestures, for they start to chatter excitedly and point at me and up at the sky.

I decide to walk back to our camp along the top instead of going down to the river again. I want to see what is between our camp and this one. Clutching my fishing net, I take my leave. I don't know how to say goodbye, so I make a little bow to the old man and then I walk slowly away.

I have only gone a short distance before I realise that some of them are following me! I turn round, and smile and beckon them. And I pray that, if they come to our camp, Wouter won't fire his musket at them.

Several young men follow me, armed with spears and narrow, decorated wooden shields. I wait for them to catch me up and I put my hand out to touch one of the shields. It is decorated with strange patterns in ochre and white, and I wonder how they have made the colours. From earth pigments? From ash?

The young men move with a loping stride that covers the ground quickly, and the sharp shale and rocks beneath their feet doesn't appear to hurt them. I find it difficult to stay in front of them, but I know I must be the one to see Wouter first. Now that I am really close to them, I am aware of their bodies and of their smell – a smell of smoke and a strong body odour which is far more pleasant than that of the stinking, unwashed men on *Batavia*.

The trees and scrub are thick here and several times I catch sight of the strange furry creatures bounding away from us in fright. It is their feeding time, before the heat of the sun forces them to rest in the shade, and I watch how they use their forepaws to tear leaves from the bushes.

We come across a thick plantation of vines

(the ones with roots beneath them) and I stop and point at them. The men stop, too, and say something to me over and over again, but I cannot understand them. There are deep holes beside the plantation and I realise that the Aborigines must go down into these sandy tunnels to harvest the roots.

What a strange, magical land this is! No one at home would believe that we have seen such sights.

We must have been going for about an hour because the sun is well up now. We come round a bend that I recognise and I know we are near our own camp. I am breathless with keeping up the pace set by the young men, but now my heart beats even faster as we approach and I slow down, putting off for as long as possible the moment when Wouter will see me – and the Aborigines. But I am proud, too, and anxious to show them our camp, so different from theirs.

As we come in sight of it, the Aborigines hang back and let me go first.

Wouter has seen us approach and he is standing at the edge of the camp, his musket pointing towards us.

'Wouter,' I shout. 'Wouter, put the musket down. These people are friendly. I have spent the night with them at their camp. They are friendly, I tell you. Look, they have given us a fishing net.' I hold it up for him to see.

Slowly he lowers the musket, but as I come up to him I can see the fear and suspicion in his eyes.

'You idiot, Jan,' he spits at me. 'You should not have left without me.'

Furious, I say quietly, 'I'm no idiot, Wouter, and I have befriended them at last.'

He does not reply, but stares at the young men who are now standing close together, their spears held at one side of their bodies and their shields at the other.

They stare back at him, and for a moment I see him through their eyes. He must appear even stranger and wilder and more frightening to them than I, for he has a great reddish beard and curly fair hair that surrounds his face like a halo. Like me, he has pale blue eyes, and now they are staring with fright.

I am used to Wouter giving me orders, but I see that, for once, he is at a loss, so I start talking to the Aborigines.

'Why are you talking to them?' hisses Wouter. 'They can't understand you.'

I ignore him, and gesture for them to sit by the fire, but they still stand in a group staring first at Wouter and then pointing at our hut and at the iron cooking pot and musket, and talking excitedly amongst themselves.

It is no wonder that they think (as I learn later) we have come from another world. They have never seen such implements before, and our hut is far sturdier than theirs.

At last Wouter snaps out of his trance. 'We should show them the trading items, Jan,' he says, and his voice is husky. 'That is what Pelsaert ordered us to do.'

Pelsaert! How long ago it all seems. I would rather not be reminded of Pelsaert, even though he spared my life.

I nod, and go into the hut to find the chest, but as I start to heave it outside, the entrance of the hut is blocked by the Aborigines all staring inside and gesturing.

I push my way through them and put the chest down on the sandy ground.

'We'll show them the toys,' says Wouter, and he kneels down and opens the clasps of the chest. One of the Aborigines leans over and touches the chest, and Wouter flinches and moves away from it.

'They are just curious,' I whisper, and I put my hand into the chest and pick up one of the colourful wooden toys – a toy soldier – and hold it out to the young man.

He backs away, grunting. But then, when I keep still, he shuffles forward again. First, he smells the toy, lowering his broad nose into my palm and then, very gingerly, he picks it up, places it between his teeth and bites it. He laughs, then, and gives it to another man to examine.

As they grow bolder, the men touch the other goods in the chest. They squat on their haunches and pick up some of the knives, chattering excitedly as they feel the sharp edges. And they laugh when I show them how the little bells ring when you shake them, but when I hold up a mirror to one of the men so that he can see his own face, he is frightened and pushes the mirror out of my hands so that it falls to the ground. I pick it up and look briefly at my own image. It is a long time since I have seen my own face. Now, at last, I am not disgusted by it.

The strings of beads are popular with them. I hold one out and show how it can be put round my neck, then I take it off and hand it to one of the men. Laughing, he puts it over his own head and they all cluster round him, admiring it.

And then, without any warning, they turn and run out of our camp, back the way they came.

I stand and look after them as they disappear. I wish they had stayed longer. I wish I could have made flour cakes for them. What will they say to the others of their tribe? How will they describe our strange implements, and what will their relations think of the little wooden toy and the string of beads?

Chapter Fourteen

Wouter

Well, we have made contact with the Aborigines at last, but their visit has made me uneasy. Jan reports that there is a sizeable family group at their camp. The young men who came to visit us were strong and they could easily have overpowered us if they wished. I saw the way they looked in awe at our hut and at some of the other goods. We must make sure that one of us is always here ready to defend our camp – with the musket, if necessary.

Jan seems to enjoy their company, stupid boy, while I still yearn for my own sort. Perhaps, soon, I shall make my way back to the shore, check on our boat and stay there a few days. If I build a fire and maybe erect some rough flagpole, I might attract the attention of a passing ship and perhaps one would come into the inlet and I could row out to it. Pelsaert, I'm sure, would be pleased to hear of what we have discovered about the natives here and the terrain. Perhaps they would even take me away ...

Yesterday, when I tried to instruct Jan in the use of the musket, he showed no interest.

'Why should we use a musket, Wouter?' he said. 'It only frightens the Aborigines, and we are learning how to hunt and forage without it. After all, they have no need of it – and see how well they manage.'

I argued with him, loaded it and tried to force it into his hands, but he flung it away.

'You can't order me about any more,' he shouted.

It was then that I realised how much he has changed in these past months. The crazed, whimpering boy – the Under Merchant's puppet – has disappeared for ever. He knows that he has skills I do not have, and this has given him courage. He seems to like the Aborigines and goes to their camp whenever he can. Unlike me, he does not crave the company of his countrymen. I don't believe he cares if he never has contact with the civilised world again!

He is happier with the savages – savages who will probably kill him.

But now that we are settled in our camp and have learnt how to feed ourselves, I am restless. I don't want to live the life of a savage.

Jan

It is some time since I first came upon the Aborigines' camp. I hoped that they would come again to visit us, but although I have been to see them again, they have not come back here.

I always go with a gift – sometimes with a catch of fish made in the net they gave me, sometimes with another string of beads from the trading chest.

I am beginning to work out who is who. The old man is the head of the family, and he and his wife have five sons. Four of the sons have wives and young children, and I believe that the girl who smiles at me is the daughter of the old man and woman, born of their old age.

The girl always knows I am coming and she is there at the edge of their camp ready to greet me, smiling and laughing and clapping her hands when I arrive, and she immediately takes whatever gift I bring and runs to her family to show them.

I try to talk to her, and we are beginning to understand each other's gestures. I think back with shame to my conduct on the island when I forced myself upon women. I would never do this to her, though my dreams are full of her – her laughing eyes and wild hair, her stocky limbs and beautiful firm breasts. I cannot help but look with longing at her nakedness, and I cannot control my dreams.

We have names for each other now. She still calls me 'Meaan', and I have made an attempt at pronouncing one of the words she says when she points at herself. I call her 'Heni'.

One day, I take a supply of the toys from the trading chest to their camp and show them how to work the wires so that the toy soldiers make a stiff, jerky, walking movement.

At first they just stare in horror, but then some of the braver ones come closer. The women seem particularly fascinated and the children, too, are wide-eyed with amazement.

Heni smiles boldly at me and I hold out one of the toys. At first, she snatches her hand away but then, laughing, she allows me to put the toy into it. She closes her fist around it and runs off to examine it.

After that, the children all crowd round me and stretch out their hands for the toys until there are no more left to give.

The young man whom I met at the river when I first came to the Aboriginal camp is the only one without a wife, and he has made himself very friendly towards me. I have named him Smiler because he is always cheerful. He laughs at my attempts to communicate with him, but he is patient and has started to teach me some useful skills.

Smiler brings his own spear for me to handle and then takes me to the trees to find a good straight branch. I watch as he rubs it smooth and selects a sharpened piece of shale, showing me how to attach it to the end of the wood.

When he has finished, he hands it to me and gestures that I am to have it. So now I have my very own spear!

I sometimes join the young men on their hunting expeditions. and I marvel at their skill.

The strange, curved wooden thing I saw on my first visit turns out to be something they throw at their prey, but I cannot master it. And the big hollowed-out tree branch is not a weapon, but a musical instrument of sorts. Often, one of the men blows into it when we are sitting round the fire and it produces a low, sad sound which echoes through the trees.

There seems to be no pattern to their hunting, except that it usually takes place at dawn or dusk. They will suddenly pick up their spears and vanish, assuming that I will follow.

I am clumsy and much slower than the others. They never wait for me so I have to keep with them, for I would get lost on my own. My feet are not as tough as theirs and bleed as we run across the unforgiving rocks and shale; I find it difficult to be as noiseless as they are when they move.

One day, I manage to spear one of the small dragon creatures and Smiler is delighted that I have added to the tribe's provisions.

Not long after this, I try to speak, with gestures, to the head of the tribe, the old man. He has not yet been to our camp and I want him to come and see for himself what the others have seen, but I can make no headway with him. At least, I think I have not, but then, one day when I am back with Wouter, the old man suddenly appears with some of his sons. He does not greet Wouter or me, but walks forward towards the fire, crouches down and starts to examine our footprints.

'What is he looking for?' asks Wouter.

I shrug. I have no more idea than Wouter.

The old man gets up slowly and approaches our hut. The young men stay back as he bends down and goes inside. When he emerges, he shakes his head, gives me a rare smile, and, refusing my offer to join us for food (which he seems to understand through my gestures) he leaves us.

Wouter is unsettled by this visit.

'We must go back to the shore and check on our boat,' he says, 'and see if we can attract the attention of a passing ship.'

I look at him in astonishment.

'But how often do Company ships come up this coast, Wouter? And even when they do, they will be miles away from the shore.'

'Pelsaert would like to know what we have found out,' says Wouter firmly. 'Maybe we can make it back to Java and report.'

'But, Wouter,' I say, scratching my head, 'Pelsaert wants us to stay here. He said so. And we are doing well. We do not want to leave now. The Aborigines will show us how to survive in the colder weather.'

Wouter shouts at me. 'I cannot live out my life among savages!'

'They are not savages!' I reply angrily.

Wouter sighs. 'I do not mean that they are without kindness, Jan, but they have no knowledge of the outside world. They have no metal, no clothes, no learning.'

'I have no learning either,' I mutter. 'Does that make me a savage?' And as soon as the words are out of my mouth, I regret them. Both Wouter and I are truly more savage than these gentle people. We are from a so-called civilized land, yet we have blood on our hands.

But Wouter isn't listening. 'We must try to get back to our own people,' he continues. 'If we can make our way to Java, we can report back to the Company all that we have seen. We shall surely be pardoned.'

I say nothing. If he tries such a mad scheme, he will be on his own, for I shall refuse to go with him.

Chapter Fifteen

Wouter

I leave Jan in charge of the camp and instruct him
to guard it.

'I shall only be gone a few days, Jan, but do
not leave the area while I am away. No visiting the
Aborigines.'

He grunts, and I suspect he won't obey me, so
I take him by the shoulders and shake him.

'I mean it, Jan! We need to protect our
property.'

He looks down at his feet and scuffs his toe in the
sandy soil.

I turn away from him, shift the full water bottle

which is strung round my neck and set off down the track. Before long, the camp is out of sight.

It is shady among the trees and I cover the ground quickly down to the waterhole. It is early and I disturb some of the furry creatures drinking there. I could have a good shot at them and instinctively my hands go to the musket slung over my shoulder, but I don't lower it.

I drink some water and take a moment to look about me, noticing how the sun's rays hit the ridge on the other side of the river and watching as its dark shape slowly becomes lighter and less menacing. It is a pretty sight.

On our first journey from the boat to the waterhole, Jan was too scared to leave my side and jumped with fear at every noise and shadow. How strange that it is he who has found it easier than I to settle here and to make friends with the Aborigines! He can survive without me now. Indeed, he can cope better than I.

I am not a fool. I know that there will, in all probability, be no ship in sight, but at least I can make myself visible if any does pass. I want to leave some clue at the shore in case another stranded sailor or soldier should be washed up here, or a ship anchor in the inlet.

As I turn away from the waterhole, something makes me look back – and I see a group of Aborigines, their spears at their sides, standing quite still on top of the ridge silhouetted against the dawn sky, watching me. They have appeared suddenly and are only dots in the distance but they are a natural part of this landscape; they belong here as surely as I do not.

Before long, I am back at the dunes where we hid the boat. It is still there, unharmed, and I feel reassured by this and sit down in the small patch of shade afforded by its bulk.

When I am rested, I take the paddle from the boat and ram it into the sand, then I strip off my shirt and attach it to the top of the paddle making a rough flag. Next, I gather firewood and light a fire. I have brought the tinderbox from our camp so that Jan will have to stay by the fire there and tend it, having no way to light it again in my absence. I smile, pleased with this ruse. He will not be able to go running off to the Aborigines.

My water bottle is full and I have some salted meat with me and three roasted roots. With luck, I should be able to find shellfish in the rock pools near the waterhole, so I shall be well fed and watered.

I have also brought the journal and quills with me and now, at last, I feel like writing something. While I am away from Jan, I can think, and I will tell what we have found here in this strange land where we have made our camp.

Slowly, I start to make my letters. I never learned much spelling but I think I can make myself understood.

Jan

As soon as Wouter is out of sight, I make for the Aboriginal camp. Wouter thinks he is so clever, taking the tinderbox. How does he think the Aborigines make their fire? They do not use a tinderbox!

This time I decide to walk by the river and climb up to their camp, just as I did the first time I discovered it.

I am hot and thirsty when I reach the river beneath their camp, so I stop for a drink and then, as there is nobody there, I strip off and wash myself. I rinse out my breeches and lay them on a rock, then settle down in the shade of a tree while the burning sun dries them.

Tired after the long walk, I fall asleep under the tree and, for once, my dreams are gentle.

I awake to the sensation of something on my skin. I jerk myself awake; I have learnt about the snakes in this country and I see how the Aborigines fear them.

But it is not a snake. I look up in horror: the Aboriginal girl is standing over me. She is giggling and letting some sandy soil trickle through her fingers and on to my naked chest. Embarrassed, I cover my genitals with my hand, jump to my feet and make my way to the rock where my breeches are drying. But as I struggle to put them on, she comes up behind me and puts her hand on my shoulder.

I turn, then, and look at her. She meets my gaze and smiles, then she puts up her hand and strokes my face.

I stop buttoning my breeches and clumsily put my hand over hers. I am not used to tenderness, and I feel a surge of such pleasure and gratitude that my eyes fill with tears.

Gently, she takes her hand from my face. She doesn't go away, but stays crouched beside me, murmuring something in her own language.

At last I gain control of myself. I sniff, and wipe my hand across my nose.

'Heni,' I say – and my voice is husky. Then I take her hand again and put it to my lips. She doesn't take it away, so I move a little closer to her. I don't want to frighten her, but I ache to have her in my arms – and to my joy she moves into my embrace naturally and happily, and we stand together, the water rushing past us.

It is I who finally tear myself away from her, and she gives a little cry. With every fibre of my body I yearn to make her my own, but I don't know what rules there are in the tribe. I respect her parents and her brothers and I don't want to offend them.

In the end, it is she who moves forward again and I am powerless to stop her. Gently she removes my breeches and strokes me. I groan, and lower her carefully to the ground, kissing her beautiful breasts and stroking her legs and buttocks. She gives herself to me with complete generosity and I am gentle in a way I have never been before, thinking of her, wanting only to give her pleasure.

When it is over, I am overwhelmed with happiness

and I hold her close to me and weep. If her father and brothers kill me now, I shall die content.

Wouter

As I sit by the boat, I think about Jan. Our relationship was never good, but it has worsened since he became involved with the Aborigines. He seems to enjoy their company in a way that I cannot and I am becoming more and more restless, more anxious to try and make contact with our own people.

For a while I had a dream of taking the boat back to Java, the two of us rowing north, but when I suggested it to Jan he said coolly, 'You go if you wish, Wouter. I shall stay here.'

'Then I shall report you,' I shouted, but the moment I said the words, I knew it was an empty threat.

He knew it, too, and laughed in my face.

I pleaded with him. 'I can't go alone, Jan, you know that. Come with me, and together we can have a great adventure – and think what we shall have to report to the Company when we reach Java!'

'It is madness,' he replied. 'We would never reach Java in that boat.'

'The Commander reached Java in an open boat,' I said.

'The longboat was large and sturdy, and the Commander had the Captain with him and a crew of sailors.'

We don't speak of it again. I know it is madness, but it is no worse than the madness that grips me here when I think of what the future holds – a future with only the boy and a lot of savages for company.

I continue to write in the journal. It is a slow business but I persevere, telling whoever may read it that we are alive, that our camp is upriver in a sandy hollow and that we have contacted the Aborigines and given them trading goods. It takes me a long time to form the words, and even then there is a deal of scratching out and rewriting.

At last I have finished, and I put the journal in the driest place I can find in the boat. Perhaps someone will read it and come looking for us. Please God that they do.

Then I heave the boat out of its hiding-place in the dunes and into full view on the shore. If a ship anchors in the inlet as the *Sardam* did, our boat will be clearly seen and someone will come to investigate.

I feel better now. I have done what I can to alert any passing ship to our presence. I will spend one more night here at the shore, straining my eyes, as I have these past three days for sight of a sail, and then I will retrace my steps and return to camp.

As the sun rises and the sea sparkles and dances in its light, I make my way along the shore, stopping to look every now and again, shading my eyes and staring towards the horizon, hoping that a sail will appear. But there is nothing. When I reach the waterhole, I turn away sadly from the sea and make my way up the path that leads to our camp.

The path is familiar now and my thoughts are miles away when I hear a rustle in the undergrowth. I stop and listen, quietly lowering my musket from my shoulder. I have disturbed one of the furry bounding creatures, and it is a little way off from me, its short forepaws held up comically before its face, regarding me.

At once I fire, hitting it cleanly. I watch as it drops stone-dead in the undergrowth, then I put the musket down on the path and stride forward. I smile as I think of the fresh meat we shall eat later.

Jan

Not for a single moment do I regret making love to Heni. 'Making love'. Those are words I never thought I would use, but that is what it was, releasing feelings in me of tenderness and affection that I didn't know I had. I can hardly believe the wonder of it, and I cannot wipe this stupid grin off my face.

Heni takes my hand and leads me up the river bank towards the Aboriginal camp, stopping from time to time to turn and smile at me and caress my arm.

It is only when we come in sight of the camp that I feel fear. What will she say – to her parents and to her brothers?

But she seems quite unconcerned as she leads me towards her father, and when she reaches him, she gestures towards me and chatters and laughs.

For a moment he looks solemn, but then his face splits into a wide smile and he reaches out and touches me.

Years later, I will learn that he considered it an honour that I – whom he believed had come from the spirit world – should have chosen his daughter.

He shouts to the rest of the family and they gather round him. There is a lot of chattering and excitement and I know it is to do with me and with Heni, but I have no idea what it all means.

When the noise has died down and the men and women settle back to what they were doing, I see that Heni's father is working on something. Timidly I creep forward to have a look. He is etching a pattern of dots and angular lines on a stout stick, and every now and then he calls one of his sons to inspect his work.

I learn later that it is a message stick which will be sent to some of the other tribes in the area, telling them of the arrival of spirit ancestors in their midst, and inviting them to come to a *corroboree*, a gathering, the lines and dots showing where and when it will be held. One of his sons will take the message stick to the other tribes.

I stay that night at their camp and take my place, as usual, by the fire, but I cannot sleep for thinking about Heni, and when everything is quiet I get up and walk to the edge of the camp, looking up at the stars and stretching my arms above my head.

I sense her presence before she is with me. And then I smell her beside me; she smells of wood smoke and of the tangy scent of the trees surrounding us. I turn towards her, holding out my arms, and we make love again on the sandy ground, slowly this time, exploring one another.

I did not think that I could feel any more love for her, but now it is even deeper and I know that I cannot leave her.

I pray that she will never find out about my past.

The next morning there is much chatter and everyone is pointing at me. I wish I knew what they were saying, for I know that they want me to do something.

At last Smiler comes up to me and gestures to me to follow him. Nervously I walk after him, away from the river and into the scrubby land beyond.

We walk until we are a good distance from the camp. Suddenly he stops, and points to a large rock. I stare at it and then back at him – then he pushes me down so that I am sitting on it. He turns to go and I get up, but he gestures at me to stay put, so I sit down again.

He seems satisfied then and lopes off back towards the camp.

The sun is hot now, and I don't know how long I can sit here. Is this some sort of punishment for making love to Heni? Or is it some sort of ritual? My mouth is dry and I have no idea what I should do.

I see Heni approaching, led by her father. As they draw closer I jump to my feet, but the old man gestures for me to sit down again. Then he presses Heni down firmly in my lap. As she sits there, he addresses her, and his words sound serious.

If it were not for Heni's smiling face, I would be frightened by this strange behaviour, but she seems completely happy and when her father turns away and retraces his steps, she jumps up and drags me to my feet.

I start to make for their camp but she pulls me in the other direction and points downriver.

And then it dawns on me. This was our marriage ceremony! Now we are man and wife and I am to take her to my camp.

Much later, I learn what her father said to her as she sat on my lap. He told her that she was not to leave me on pain of being speared!

Chapter Sixteen

Heni has not been to our camp before and I watch her face carefully as she inspects it, running first to the cold ashes of the fire, making clicks of disapproval, then touching the iron pan and the other implements – which are strange to her – before finally approaching the hut. She stands staring at it for a while, taking in its sturdiness, so different from those at her family's camp; then, timidly, she creeps inside. I stand at the entrance and watch as she picks up our blankets and feels them, frowning.

At last she emerges. She smiles at me and claps her hands in delight, then points meaningfully at the fire which I've let die, and disappears into the trees for a moment, coming back with two straight sticks and a bundle of dry leaves. I watch as she puts the leaves in the cold ash and rubs the sticks together, frowning with effort. At last, there is a spark from the friction and the dry leaves catch fire. Soon we have a merry blaze.

As the fire burns, I stare into the flames and think about Wouter. He will be angry when he finds Heni here but I shall stand up to him and explain that, in the eyes of Heni's family, we are married, and that I cannot leave her. I look round the camp. Maybe I can build a second hut for Wouter or maybe we can construct another camp.

My stomach lurches as I think of Wouter.

That night, Heni won't go inside the hut to sleep. We curl up in each other's arms beside the fire.

The next day, I busy myself showing Heni how to use the iron pan and how the spade digs the soil. She watches me carefully, but she won't try to use either of these unfamiliar implements, even when I go and dig out more roots just to show her how useful a spade can be.

Wouter has been gone for two nights and the longer he is away, the more I dread his return.

That evening, I offer Heni some salted meat

but, having smelt it, licked at it and chewed a piece, she spits it out and will only eat roots. How stupid of me to think that she will change her habits.

Early the next morning, I take the net to set it up in the river. At once she gets up and follows me. She squats at the river's edge watching as I select rocks to anchor the net. She is not pleased with what I've done and starts pointing, so I gesture to her to show me what she means. Immediately she jumps up and wades into the water.

But just as she is showing me, there is a loud bang.

Wouter's musket!

I tense. Heni splashes back to me, her eyes wide with terror, and flings herself into my arms. I hold her tight and feel the thumping of her heart, but I keep smiling and telling her there is nothing to fear, even though I am fearful. Wouter must have shot a creature at the waterhole – and that means he will soon be back at the camp.

But he does not come. All day I listen for his footfalls, for the giveaway sound of snapping twigs and tuneless whistling. But there is nothing.

Later in the day, Heni helps me take the fish we have caught and stun them on the rocks, and she cooks them on the fire. But I cannot enjoy our meal together. I am listening out all the time for Wouter.

And still he does not come. Two more days and nights go by, and I am more and more uneasy.

Smiler comes to visit us and we are both glad to see him. He holds his spear in one hand and one of the strange dragon creatures in the other. He hands it to Heni, who immediately skins and puts it in the hot ashes to cook.

He stays with us all day. This is the first time that I have seen him on his own, and I try hard to communicate with him. I point to the fire, the trees, his spear, parrots, the hut. He repeats the words for these basic things again and again, and I say them back to him. He and Heni laugh at my feeble efforts.

When the sun sets he does not leave us, but settles down by the fire to sleep. It is then, for the first time, that Heni lets me take her into the hut to lie under our blankets.

Another day dawns, and still there is no Wouter. Has something happened to him? I am filled with foreboding and I know that I must go and look for him.

I try and explain this to Smiler and Heni.

I draw the outline of a man in the sand – a primitive figure with stick arms and legs and a head covered with wild hair and a profuse beard, then I point in the direction of the waterhole, pick up my water bottle and set off through the trees.

I still have not learned how to walk quietly as the Aborigines do, and I am conscious of my clumsiness. Some sixth sense alerts me to the fact that I am being followed, and I turn round to see Smiler a little distance behind me. He stops when I look back and stands still, resting on his spear. I smile and beckon to him, grateful for his presence.

As we approach the waterhole, I catch sight of the musket lying abandoned on the path. Instinctively, I crouch down beside it and as I do so, Smiler touches my shoulder and gestures towards the undergrowth.

His sharp eyes have spotted what I have missed.

Slowly I get to my feet and follow his gaze. At first, because the trees cast shadows over the dense tangle of ferns beneath them, I can see nothing. But then I make out a shape and, as my eyes adjust to the gloom, I see that it is the pale skin of a man's back.

I start forward with a cry, but Smiler hauls me back by my arm. I look at him in anguish, but still he holds me, and each time I try to move, he shouts at me. Then, with his spear, he bangs the ground, before walking slowly forwards, and this time he does not stop me as I follow him.

Wouter is slumped over the corpse of a furry creature. I stand rooted to the spot, as Smiler turns his body over, grunting with the effort.

The ants have already been at him and his face is not a pretty sight. I turn away, retching, but Smiler, after banging his spear again on the ground, kneels down beside the body and carefully examines it. I cannot bear to look, and it is not until Smiler grabs my arm, chattering and pointing, that I turn back. Smiler is touching Wouter's leg with his finger.

Just above the ankle I see a tiny puncture mark and all around it the skin is swollen and bloated. I stare at the wound and nod, even as Smiler makes a swirling gesture with his hand. And at last I understand what he is trying to tell me. Wouter has been bitten by a snake and the venom has killed him.

I never felt grief for any of the poor souls on the islands as I now feel for Wouter. A long moaning cry comes from within me and I stand there, helpless, above the empty husk of the man who has been my constant companion these past months.

But Smiler already has his hands under Wouter's

armpits, and drags him through the undergrowth and back on to the path. Then he squats down and, with astonishing strength, heaves the corpse over his shoulder and stands up.

He is about to start back to our camp, but I stop him.

I don't know how the Aborigines bury their dead, but I am certain that Wouter would not like to be buried with their rites. So I point down towards the shore and walk forward, numb with misery. Some instinct is making me head for the sea where I feel his last resting-place should be. I scarcely know what I have in mind until we reach the shore, and I indicate to Smiler that we should walk along the sand. We stop frequently so that Smiler can rest. He is not smiling now, and his face is grim with effort. I give him water from my bottle and offer to take a turn at carrying Wouter, but Smiler won't let me and I am grateful for his strength and his trust.

It is only when I see the boat that I know what I shall do – what Wouter would want me to do. It lies out in full view and beside it Wouter has made a rustic flag-pole from the paddle and his shirt.

I help Smiler lift Wouter's body into the boat and, as I do so, I see the journal tucked in the stern. I take it out and notice that Wouter has added some more scribblings. For a while I hold it, wondering whether I should keep it, but at last I put it back where Wouter has hidden it.

No one will read it now.

I stare out to sea. The tide is going out. I start to heave the boat towards the water and Smiler helps me. Slowly, slowly, inch by inch, we push the boat until at last it is bobbing in the water.

We thrust it out into the waves until we can no longer stand up. Then we let it go, and watch it as it swirls about in the current.

I cannot remember any of the preacher's prayers and, in any case, they don't seem right in this place, so I send my thoughts with Wouter and commit him to the wind and tide.

I would like to think that the boat will be swept up the coast and make landfall in Java, taking Wouter back to a place where there are people of his own race, but I know that it will simply be tossed about in the rips, dashed upon coral or rocks and sink to the bottom of the sea, taking Wouter and the journal with it.

I no longer need a boat of this kind. If I ever make a boat, it will be a canoe like the one I saw when I had my first sight of an Aborigine.

Smiler and I watch as the little boat swirls and bobs in the water. We stand together looking after it until it is just a smudge on the horizon.

Then I wrench the boat's upright paddle from the sand, untie Wouter's shirt and bury my head in it, breathing the scent of his body. Smiler stands apart from me as I weep into its folds.

As I stumble back along the shore, I think of Wouter: a rough soldier, to be sure, and a man who didn't hesitate to kill – or to lead the other mutineers when Corneliez was captured – but I shall always remember his kindness. I shall remember the way he protected Lucretia, how he helped me smear ointment on my sore hands and bind them with strips of shirt, how he took charge when we arrived here.

I take one last look at the sea before we strike up the path towards the camp. As we pass the waterhole, I pause briefly at the corpse of the furry creature, but I do not want it. If Wouter had not shot it and disturbed a snake as he went to pick it up, he would still be alive today.

Now, the only connection with my past life is gone. It was a life in which I endured misery and ridicule and I have no desire to return to it. As one day follows another, I forget more and more and relax into the rhythm of living here with Heni. Her simplicity, her openness and her tenderness towards me enchant me.

Epilogue

All this happened long ago. As time passed, I learnt the Aboriginal language and how to hunt turtles, birds and frogs. I learnt which plants are good to eat. I learnt, too, of the Aborigines' beliefs: how the ancestor spirits came to earth and formed the people, the land, the plants and animals; how Beemarra, the rainbow serpent, formed the rivers and hills with its body, and how its scales scraped off to form the forests and flowers.

When I understood this, I began to interpret the stories of the spirit ancestors retold through dances and ceremonies performed at the *corroborees* when different tribes came together and traded shells at the river's edge. I began to understand, too, the significance of secret rituals and rites – men's business and women's business.

But for years I did not realise that Heni's family thought I was a spirit ancestor returned to them. This was why they accepted our union and even gave me my own territory, so that I could pass it on to my sons.

Our first child – a boy – has Heni's features but his skin is paler than hers and he has my fair hair and blue eyes. We named him after the Aboriginal god Nogomain, who gives spirit children to mortal parents.

Many years later, long after our children were grown up, we received a special message stick which, for the first time in years, reminded me of my past life. I am now expert at interpreting the lines and dots upon these sticks. But this message stick was unwelcome. It told of more ancestor spirits who had come to these shores – in large numbers – and I guessed that there had been another shipwreck and that more Dutch sailors had arrived. But when I read the signs more carefully, I saw that these 'spirit ancestors' had been seen many miles south of us.

For some years I feared that these sailors might venture up the coast to our river, and I dreaded meeting them, for they would have heard of *Batavia's* shipwreck and of the mutiny and the massacre. They would know that Wouter and I had been marooned on this coast. But, although I waited for other message sticks that might bring news of them, none ever came.

I am old now and near death, but death holds no fear for me. It is only the first step into the spirit world.

Heni is beside me. Like me, she is old and toothless, but our affection for each other has never wavered.

We hear the sound of laughter and we see the men come in from hunting, noisy with success. Our three sons are in front, leading the way into the camp.

Three strong, blue-eyed Aborigines.

Historical note

On October 28th 1628, the Dutch East India Company ship *Batavia* sailed from Texel, an island off the north coast of Holland, on her maiden voyage to Batavia (present-day Jakarta) in Java. The ship was laden with a priceless cargo including jewels, silver coins and *objets d'art* to be traded for highly prized spices. Francisco Pelsaert, an employee of the Dutch East India Company, was in command of the ship and Jeronimus Corneliez, another Company employee, was second-in-command. However, neither of these well-educated men knew how to sail a ship and responsibility for this lay with the skipper, Ariaen Jacobsz. But his authority could be countermanded at any time by the two company men.

Jacobsz had sailed with Pelsaert on a previous voyage and despised him, so the relationship between Captain and Commander was not a happy one.

There were 316 people on board *Batavia*. As well as troops for the colonies and sailors, cramped in the squalid lower decks, there were passengers, many of them destitute and hoping for a better life away from their native Holland. A few, however, were wealthy and these passengers were housed in the relative comfort of the cabins astern.

When the ship docked at Cape Town, Captain Jacobsz went on a violent drinking spree and Commander Pelsaert rebuked him publicly, which made the relationship between Captain and Commander worse than ever.

The second-in-command, Under Merchant Jeronimus Corneliez, had joined the company as a last resort, to avoid being arrested at home in Holland. His career as an apothecary was ruined and his creditors had uncovered his association with an heretical sect which believed that sin did not exist. This religious affiliation goes some way to explain his chilling detachment and lack of self-blame during the events on the island. He was also manipulative, persuasive and charismatic, exerting power over his followers and bending them to his will.

Jacobsz and Corneliez formed a dangerous alliance and they began to plan a mutiny, intending to seize the ship and her valuable cargo, kill the Commander and those loyal to him and then live as pirates. They gathered about them some hot-headed cadets and discontented sailors and directed them to attack the Commander's friend, a high-born young woman, Lucretia van der Meylen, who was on her way to join her husband in Batavia. Jacobsz and Corneliez were sure that the Commander would react violently to this act, and his retaliation would be the signal for the mutiny to begin.

In the event, Pelsaert did not lash out as expected, remaining passive and reasonable. Lucretia could only identify one of her attackers and he was imprisoned on board to await trial on the mainland.

So, the lid was on the mutiny – but only just – when *Batavia* ran aground on Morning Reef off the Houtman Abrolhos Islands (near Geraldton, Western Australia) on June 4th, 1629.

The Mutiny and after

The details of *Batavia's* ill-fated voyage and the subsequent events on the islands were all meticulously recorded by Commander Francisco Pelsaert. He died in 1630, broken and disgraced, a year after the shipwreck. The captain of *Batavia,* Ariaen Jacobsz, died in prison while awaiting trial in Java. Wiebbe Hayes, however, came out well from the mutiny. He went from ordinary soldier to commissioned officer, receiving a substantial pay rise, and on his return to Batavia (Jakarta) he was promoted even further in recognition of his deeds by the Council for the Indies.

Jan Pelgrom's crimes are listed as the murder of a cabin boy and assisting in two other murders, as well as 'misbehaving with married women'.

Wouter Looes' crimes are listed as taking part in the killing of the preacher's family and of commanding the mutineers after the capture of Corneliez.

In 1656 the *Vergulde Draeck* (Gilt Dragon) was wrecked off Cape Leschenault, much further south from the wreck site of *Batavia.* It is known that at least seventy-five survivors reached the shore and that seven of these sailed for Java. The remaining sixty-eight were never seen again, at least not by subsequent rescue parties.

Jan and Wouter are remembered, not for their crimes, but because they were the first white men to have lived on the continent of Australia.

Sightings

The first specific report of an Aboriginal with European characteristics in Western Australia was in May 1836 (seven years after European settlement in the region). George Moore encountered 'a young woman of a very pleasing countenance and something of European features and long, wavy, almost flaxen-coloured hair.' Perth Gazette, 1836.

In 1839, Lieutenant George Grey wrote: 'We passed two native villages, the huts of which they were composed differed from those in the southern districts, in being built, and very nicely plastered over the outside with clay, and clods of turf... they were evidently intended for fixed places of residence.' This suggests that the Nanda people of the Western coastal regions might have absorbed some Dutch building techniques. The area where Grey saw the villages was close to '*warran* grounds' – *warran* being the edible root favoured by the Nanda people – and close to the mouth of the Hutt River where it is thought likely that Jan and Wouter were marooned. For the purposes of this book, I have assumed that the *warran* grounds were established when Jan and Wouter were marooned, but it is possible that the yams were introduced by early Dutch settlers.

In 1848, the explorer Augustus Charles Gregory reported: 'I explored the country where the mutineers had landed and found a tribe whose character differed considerably from the average Aborigine. Their colour was neither black nor copper, but that peculiar colour that prevails with a mixture of European blood.'

Daisy May Bates, an Irish Australian journalist (1859-1951) and lifelong student of Australian Aboriginal culture and society, recognised European features in Aboriginals of the Western Australian coastal tribes: 'I also found traces of types distinctly Dutch. When Pelsaert marooned two white criminals on the mainland of Australia these Dutchmen had probably been allowed to live with the natives, and it may be that they are their progeny... there was no mistaking the flat heavy Dutch face, curly fair hair, and heavy, stocky build.' *The Passing of the Aborigines,* (Panther, London, 1966).

Lastly, 'The first white men to settle did so reluctantly as they were the two sailors of the *Batavia* marooned for their part in the mutiny of 1629, which could account for the natives with fair hair and blue eyes reported by our pioneers.'

The Shire of Northampton, Western Australia, A.C. Henville (Geraldton Newspaper Ltd, 1968).

At the time of going to press, initial DNA tests have confirmed that some Aboriginals from Western Australia carry Western European blood. Further tests should allow researchers to pinpoint the date when that genetic link came about and whether it predated British settlement.

Bibliography

Batavia's Graveyard, Mike Dash (Weidenfeld & Nicholson, 2002).

The Accomplice, Kathryn Heyman (Headline Book Publishing, 2003).

And Their Ghosts May be Heard, Rupert Gerritsen (Fremantle Arts Centre Press, 2002).

Acknowledgements

My thanks to Mike Lefroy of the Western Australian Maritime Museum for invaluable information and advice.

Rosemary Hayes

lives and works in Cambridgeshire.
She has written numerous books for children
including historical and contemporary fiction
and fantasy. Rosemary lived in Australia for six
years, and her first children's novel *Race Against
Time*, set in Australia, was runner-up for the
Kathleen Fidler Award. Rosemary's first Frances
Lincoln book, *Mixing It*, about the relationship
between a Muslim girl and a non-Muslim boy
against a background of terrorism, was shortlisted
for the South Lanarkshire Book Award.
Her next book, *Payback*, was based on the
actual experiences of a young Muslim
woman who was brave enough to defy
her family and reject the husband
chosen for her.

More books by Rosemary Hayes

MIXING IT

Fatimah is a devout Muslim. Steve is a regular
guy who's never given much thought to faith.
Both happen to be in the same street the day
a terrorist bomb explodes. Steve is badly
injured and when the emergency services arrive,
Fatimah has bandaged his shattered leg and is
cradling his head in her lap, willing him to stay
alive. But the Press is there too, and their picture
makes the front page of every newspaper.
'Love across the divide,' scream the headlines.
Then the anonymous 'phone calls start.
Can Steve and Fatimah rise above the hatred
and learn to understand each other? But while
they are breaking down barriers, the terrorists
have another target in mind...

Praise for *Mixing It*:

"A tense thriller set against
a background of terrorism."
Cambridge Evening News

"A topical and well-researched book."
Bookfest

"Full of insight into the plight
of young Muslims, trapped, as they
see it, between their love of life in secular
Britain and their loyalty to a faith
developed long ago in distant lands."
Church Times

PAYBACK

Halima has her whole life to look forward to.
Brought up in a Pakistan village and now
settled in London with her family, her horizons
are widening all the time. She is starting
university in London and she has met
a Muslim boy she really likes.

And then she discovers her father's plan –
to marry her to the son of a distant relation
in Pakistan who once did him a favour.
Halima is to be the repayment of a debt,
and it's payback time.